Praise For
Bob Balaban's
McGROWL #1:
BEWARE OF DOG

"Mr. Balaban takes his obvious love of language and wordplay and creates a magical tale of a mind-reading dog that all young minds should read. An intelligent and plentiful debut."
— *Jamie Lee Curtis*

"For anybody who has ever had a dog, loved a dog, or wanted a dog. A great adventure beautifully written. I hope Bob writes the next one about me."
— *Richard Dreyfuss*

#1

BEWARE OF DOG

Bob Balaban

A Storyopolis Book

AN
APPLE
PAPERBACK

SCHOLASTIC INC.
New York Toronto London Auckland Sydney
Mexico City New Delhi Hong Kong Buenos Aires

No part of this publication may be reproduced in whole or in part, or stored in a retrieval system, or transmitted in any form or by any means, electronic, mechanical, photocopying, recording, or otherwise, without written permission of the publisher. For information regarding permission, write to Scholastic Inc., Attention: Permissions Department, 557 Broadway, New York, NY 10012.

ISBN 0-439-40137-2

STORYOPOLIS is a multifaceted entertainment company dedicated to celebrating and preserving the visual, oral, and written tradition of stories in all forms of media. Through our unique art gallery and bookstore based in Los Angeles, STORYOPOLIS features the finest in creation in illustrated children's books and picture book art and provides both children and adults with the resources to "feed the mind and soul."

www.STORYOPOLIS.com

12 11 10 9 8   2 3 4 5 6 7/0
                                              40
Printed in the U.S.A.
First Scholastic printing, August 2002

For Mariah and Hazel,
who never had a dog.
Yet.
— B. B.

Contents

CHAPTER ONE
The Adventure Begins

"Thomas Wiggins, you are not leaving this house until you put every single thing back in that drawer and comb your hair."

Thomas looked up sheepishly at his mother, who had appeared out of nowhere and planted herself firmly in the doorway.

Thomas had just assembled a backpack full of wire and string and some other useful-looking stuff from the special kitchen drawer where his mother kept an assortment of things that didn't belong anywhere else. "I'm waiting." She tapped her foot and folded her arms across her chest.

Thomas quickly did his best to restore order to the drawer, ran his hands through the tangle of wavy brown hair that fell onto his forehead, and picked up his backpack. And then he tried to make it outside before his mother thought of anything else for him to do. He was at least fifteen minutes late for Violet, his best and only friend. Violet lived across the street and three houses down the block and didn't like to be kept waiting.

"And don't forget to be back in plenty of time for dinner," Thomas's mother called after him.

By now Thomas had made it out the door, across the lawn, and onto the sidewalk. He looked up at the sky, which was turning an ominous shade of greenish gray, but decided not to risk going back for an umbrella. Mrs. Wiggins could turn a chance of bad weather into a doomsday scenario that might require not only galoshes but hats and gloves and scarves as well. He decided he'd rather risk a couple of raindrops. After all, he was a year older now.

His birthday had been two days ago, a fact that seemed to hold enormous importance for his mother. Frankly, Thomas wasn't so sure being one year older was going to have a significant impact on anything. It had been a perfectly fine party. Violet Schnayerson and her older sister, Alicia, and their parents came. Thomas's older brother, Roger, managed to stay until dinner was served before rushing off to basketball practice. And of course, Thomas's parents were there.

Mr. Wiggins was supposed to make an important business trip to Cleveland that evening, but he managed to postpone it, and Mrs. Wiggins baked an unbelievably delicious cake that was an exact replica of the Wiggins's house. It had two stories, a tidy red-shingled roof, and adorable dormer windows with panes of glass made out of melted lollipops. The cake sat on a perfect lawn made of green spun sugar, in the middle of which Mrs. Wiggins spelled out HAPPY BIRTHDAY, THOMAS. She had managed to whip it up somewhere in between her eighteenth-century European decorative arts study group and her aerobics class.

It was generally acknowledged that there was very little Mrs. Wiggins couldn't do, but even she seemed proud and excited as she emerged from the kitchen with her amazing creation. Thomas closed his eyes as he made the wish he had been making for as many birthdays as he was able to remember.

He tried to concentrate his thoughts into a tiny pinpoint that might actually help make his wish come true. *I wish for a dog, I wish for a dog, I wish for a dog, I wish for a dog.* Then he gently blew out the candles, careful not to get wax on any of the flowers. He even imagined for a second that his wish was coming true, and he thought he could hear the sound of tiny paws scurrying in from the other room. But when he opened his eyes he wasn't terribly surprised to find a small collection of neatly wrapped gifts, and not a canine in sight.

This was, after all, just another ordinary birthday and not the miraculous beginning of what Thomas was looking forward to as his "dog years." When he thought of time, which was frequently, he divided it into BD and AD: Before Dog and After Dog. He had to admit BD was beginning to look like a permanent condition.

Before Thomas could talk, he loved dogs. When Mrs. Thompson's black Labrador, Ralph, would come careening into the playground, sending small children flying with a wave of his immense tail, even the bravest of the older toddlers would run to their mothers or baby-sitters for protection. Thomas would try to get closer so he could give the dog a hug.

Ralph seemed genuinely fond of Thomas. The imposing-looking animal never even barked at him and tried really hard not to knock him down. In return, Thomas never grabbed at his fur like the other children did. He seemed to know instinctively that dogs didn't want you to scream in their ears and needed to be scratched on top of their heads and on their bellies and in other places their paws couldn't reach.

Even Mrs. Wiggins had to admit that Thomas had a special way with animals. She herself didn't exactly mind dogs, she just didn't have much use for them. Even the neatest of dogs could mess up your house in record time. And when you wanted to take that last-minute vacation to, say, the restored village of Williamsburg, Virginia, you could never find anybody to take care of them. Pets, Thomas's mother had long ago decided, were simply not in the cards.

Mr. Wiggins, oddly enough, was afraid of dogs. Although he was over six feet tall and not likely to be referred to as slim, he had a hard time looking them in the eye. When he did, he imagined they were plotting clever ways to sneak up on him and bite him. Put simply, Mr. Wiggins was even less inclined than Mrs. Wiggins ever to allow an animal inside the house.

Violet was sitting on the curb, counting her allowance, when she heard Thomas approach at last. She breathed a little sigh of relief.

"Thought you'd never get here," she said.

"You and me both," Thomas volunteered.

"Trouble on the home front?" asked Violet.

Thomas seriously pondered the question, thought of a reply, thought better of it, forgot the question altogether, and started thinking about the many uses of waxed paper. None of this caused him to slow down.

"Think it's gonna rain?" she ventured.

Thomas looked up at the sky, which was definitely looking ominous, and said, "Earthworms."

"Excuse me?" Violet tried not to seem surprised. Thomas's answers didn't always match the questions.

"Perfect day for earthworms," Thomas explained.

And Violet realized that was Thomas's way of telling her that yes, it was going to rain, because earthworms would surface from their underground holes and crevices to avoid being drowned. Thomas loved earthworms.

As Violet tried to catch up with him, she smoothed out the rumpled denim dress she had worn to her grandmother's house that morning. She had decided not to take the time to change. Thomas was just as likely to be early as he was to be late, and she didn't want to miss him.

Thomas was glad that Violet had waited for him. She never seemed to notice the awkward silences that punctuated his attempts at conversation the way the other kids did. And she seemed genuinely to look forward to their afternoons together. She understood that best friends didn't have to say a lot or even be popular. You just had to like them.

So off they trudged, past rows of freshly painted houses standing neatly at attention behind newly mowed lawns.

"What did you think of the math quiz yesterday?" Violet asked.

"Didn't finish," Thomas confessed.

"How come?"

He seriously considered the question for longer than Violet would have thought possible and said simply, "Got involved." Thomas occasionally found the math questions too easy and spent the time dreaming up more challenging ones.

The wind was pushing at their backs as, high above them, storm clouds lined up across an ever-darkening sky. They took the shortcut through the empty lot behind the big stone house that was commonly referred to as the old witch's castle and encountered some kids from Thomas's class. They didn't seem to notice him approaching, which was not unusual.

Once somebody at school had said that Thomas was so quiet you couldn't tell if he was dead or alive, and a rumor had circulated that Thomas actually was dead. For several days people pretended not to notice him and acted as if he wasn't there. It wasn't particularly upsetting to Thomas, since finding things to say to his classmates was never easy for him. Nor was there an enormous difference in the way they treated him when they weren't going around pretending he was dead.

BEWARE OF DOG

Sides were being chosen for a game of pickup baseball. Thomas at once spotted Lewis Musser. Lewis was the biggest boy in fifth grade. He didn't especially dislike Thomas. Lewis just treated him like he treated all the other boys in the class who were smaller than he was, which was everybody, which was like his personal slave.

Lewis had perfected the fine art of getting people to treat him as if he were king without exactly threatening to flatten them, although that possibility certainly existed. Thomas frequently did Lewis's homework for him. Sometimes he would even sign in for Lewis when Lewis was late for school in the morning because he was busy skateboarding and couldn't make it to first period. That's what you did with Lewis. Lewis's father owned half of Cedar Springs, and Lewis felt he could pretty much get away with anything. And he was pretty much right.

Thomas looked down, felt nervously in his pockets, and before anyone had a chance to notice him pretended he must have left something at home and quickly doubled back. He and Violet would take the long way to the wooded area that ran across the north end of town.

Storm clouds rumbled faintly in the distance as Thomas and Violet waited patiently at the intersection for the light to change.

"A six-letter word meaning cheap or flashy." Violet was always trying to find a word Thomas didn't know. So far this had not been possible.

"Easy," Thomas replied. "Tawdry." A couple of raindrops landed smack in the middle of his glasses, and he looked up ruefully at the ever-darkening sky. He had to admit he wasn't entirely happy about his decision not to return for the umbrella. They crossed the street and started down the path that led to the little ravine where Thomas performed experiments with water and sand and bits of leaves. He liked to classify the rocks he found there. He had spent many hours talking to Violet about things like the difference between igneous and bituminous and why baking soda was one of the miracles of the modern world.

Thomas put his collar up high around his neck, and Violet wound her sweater around her as a tightly as she could. The temperature was definitely dropping quickly, but neither was about to admit defeat and head for home. Thomas carefully laid his backpack down on a rock, and Violet helped him arrange the small collection of tools he had gathered from the kitchen.

"We've gotta be really careful," said Thomas. "That's my mother's favorite spoon."

Violet was only half listening. She glanced up at the sky, which was turning darker every second. She tried not to notice that the wind was sending a steady stream of leaves and dust whirling around their heads.

"Darn it," Thomas said as the prized spoon folded in upon itself. "There's just too much granite over here."

"Maybe we should go home," Violet suggested hopefully.

Thomas, completely absorbed, ignored her and hummed an aimless little tune while poking away at the dirt. A flash of lightning was followed by a crack of thunder so loud Violet rubbed her ears, and still Thomas dug and dug. She counted the number of seconds that elapsed between the lightning and the thunder and came up with two. She couldn't remember whether that meant the lightning was two miles away or two blocks away. In either case, it was definitely time to run for cover. She gave an involuntary shudder.

Suddenly, it got very quiet, and the wind settled down. Thomas seemed to notice something. He froze. He stopped what he was doing, lifted his head up, and looked around so intently that the hair on Violet's neck stood on end. Something was about to happen that would change their lives forever, and she knew it. And then her friend spoke. Carefully and quietly and very, very gently.

"Here, boy. Don't be afraid. It's okay, no one's going to hurt you."

He sounded confident and secure, and Violet felt reassured by the tone in his voice. She looked in the direction of Thomas's gaze. It was getting so dark that at first she didn't see the big, shaggy dog staring back at them. She heard his gentle breathing and noticed the glint of something metallic attached to his collar. But the shape of the animal itself was hard to distinguish from the murky background of leaves and rocks against which he was standing.

Thomas didn't take his eyes from the dog

for a second, and the dog stared right back at Thomas. After a few moments that seemed more like hours, the dog made a sound a little like a whimper but more like a sigh and tilted his head to one side.

Thomas knew a few things right away. The dog was intelligent, the dog was friendly, and the dog was lost.

CHAPTER TWO
A New Friend

"Let's get you something to eat," said Thomas.

Thomas found the presence of the dog so thrilling he could barely contain himself. He tried to remain calm as he searched his pockets for something to offer the hungry-looking animal. The dog's ribs were sticking out, and he looked like he hadn't had anything to eat for a long time, but he didn't seem particularly unhappy. In fact, although his canine research indicated such a thing was hardly possible, it occurred to Thomas that the dog was smiling at him.

All Thomas could find were a couple of used tissues and some paper clips. He dug deeper and located a Snickers wrapper. Lewis Musser had taken the actual bar during one of the prelunchtime raids he regularly made on Thomas's lunch box. Thomas had gotten so hungry during recess yesterday that he had used his teeth to scrape off every molecule of the chocolate that remained on the wrapper. He doubted that even the faintest aroma of Snickers still lingered there.

The dog certainly was curious. He took a tentative step forward to get a better look at whatever it was Thomas was holding and panted expectantly.

"He's really hungry," Thomas said under his breath. "You got anything?"

Thomas looked desperately over at Violet, who managed to locate half a lollipop she had tucked away for emergencies. If this wasn't an emergency, she thought, then what was? She brushed away some pocket fuzz that clung to its edges and carefully handed it over. The dog followed her every movement.

"You think he likes root beer?" Violet whispered.

"It's worth a try," Thomas replied.

Thomas took the candy, knelt down, and held it out to the dog. "Here you go," he said nonchalantly. He wished his hand would stop trembling.

The dog sniffed the air and then inched his way closer and closer until Thomas could feel his breath on his open palm. "Don't be afraid, it's okay."

In a flash, the dog gobbled up the lollipop and started madly licking Thomas's hand. Thomas let out a giggle. And then the dog jumped up on him and started licking his face, and Thomas, who was hunkering down, completely lost his balance. He fell backward, and the dog hopped up on him and continued licking away. It was Violet's turn to giggle. She leaned over and patted the matted fur that stuck up all over the dog's head. The animal gave her a couple of thank-you licks and then went back to attacking Thomas. Clearly, the dog was crazy about the kid.

Thomas tried desperately to control the thoughts that were racing through his head. Was this, at long last, the beginning of AD? His head swam with pictures of dogs. Dogs who slept under your bed at night, and dogs who followed you to school in the morning. Dogs who went to the dentist with you and sat on your lap so you wouldn't notice the drilling so much.

True, the animal didn't resemble any of the photos of collies and Border terriers and Samoyeds and Portuguese water dogs that crowded the walls of Thomas's bedroom. But he did have a certain noble beauty if you could see beneath the tangle of mud and leaves that clung to his fur. And anyway, the dog's appearance was absolutely immaterial to him. If Thomas was ever to have a dog — his own dog — a dog who lived in his house, in his room, on his bed — it would surely have to be a dog very much like the one who was currently trying to burrow his head under his arm.

But Thomas forced himself to think about the person who was at this very moment probably running all over town putting up pictures of this lost dog and offering a large reward for his return. What if the owner were a child? A boy exactly like Thomas?

The feeling was almost too much for him to bear. Thomas knew what he had to do. He struggled to his feet. The dog ran around him two or three times and dashed deeper into the woods. Then, just as quickly, he ran back to Thomas and Violet, letting them know that if they were any kind of playmates at all they would follow him.

Thomas spoke quietly and firmly. "He belongs to somebody, and we've got to find his owner."

Violet tried to get the dog to stand still while Thomas struggled to read the writing on the metal tag that dangled from his expensive-looking collar.

"Hold still, boy," Thomas urged. The tag was shaped like a heart that had been torn in half. Thomas imagined that its ragged edge matched the edge of its missing partner. The lettering was faint, but Thomas thought he could make out the word *Friends*, engraved in a delicate, curving style.

He searched in his backpack for the piece of carbon paper he saved for just such moments and began rubbing it against some faded scratches below the engraving. Violet remembered a book she had read last year about a young detective. Daphne, as she was called, once rubbed carbon paper against a similarly faded engraving to reveal the secrets of a lost tribe of Indians. She wondered what amazing mystery the tag was about to reveal.

Thomas rubbed harder. A five-digit number began to emerge. First a three, then two zeros, then a two, and then a four: 30024.

"I wonder if that's his age in dog years," Violet said thoughtfully.

"Must be the zip code. Let's get going," Thomas muttered as they headed off in the direction from which they had just come.

The dog hesitated a moment, as if weighing a terribly important decision — which indeed he was — and then raced after Thomas and Violet, barking happily.

Thomas tried to imagine under what circumstances such a fantastic animal could have found himself separated from his owner and so far from home. Thomas's dreaded dentist lived in the 30023 zip code, and that was at least a forty-five-minute bus ride away.

"What are we gonna do with him if we can't find the owner? Your mom won't even let him in the house." Violet certainly had the knack of getting right to the heart of the matter.

"We'll have to look really hard," Thomas replied. But Violet's question troubled him deeply.

What, indeed, Thomas wondered, would he do with the dog if the owner could not be located?

How on earth would he ever convince his parents to let him have a pet? His mother had made him a list of rules a mile long when she thought he might possibly win a goldfish at the third-grade carnival. He didn't even win the fish, but his mother still insisted on keeping the rules taped to the back of his closet door.

BEWARE OF DOG

Thomas became so preoccupied that he failed to notice he was back at the witch's castle. The game had just broken up, and Lewis and two of his pals were hanging out, looking for short boys to order around. Violet tried to nudge Thomas discreetly. Too late. Lewis had already spotted him.

"Your lunch was really good yesterday, Timothy, but could you tell your mom to go easy on the Snickers bars? I'm thinking of losing a couple of pounds."

"His name is Thomas. Not Timothy," said Violet. Violet tried to sound polite but not too wishy-washy. She longed for someone to finally stand up to Lewis and put an end to his tyrannical reign.

"Whatever," Lewis casually replied. "Anybody feel like carrying my duffel bag home? I'm pretty tired." The request really didn't sound threatening, Thomas observed, it just had a persuasive quality to it. In fact, Thomas had already started running around gathering up stray mitts and bats and balls and putting them into the bag when Lewis said the thing he said. He didn't even mean anything by it. Really, it was just the kind of stuff he was always saying so that everybody would keep thinking he was really cool. But this time he had gone too far.

"That's a really useless-looking dog," Lewis said, gesturing at the scruffy animal.

"You better not say anything bad about my dog or I'll hurt you," said Thomas, staring Lewis straight in the eyes.

Violet's jaw dropped, and she looked at Thomas in disbelief. Thomas himself was pretty shocked at the words that had tumbled, unplanned, from his mouth. Even the dog seemed to notice something out of the ordinary was going on.

Lewis looked at Thomas strangely and then

asked Violet, almost as if he really cared, "Is he all right?"

Everybody waited nervously to see what Lewis was going to do to Thomas. It was clear he wasn't going to take this threat lying down.

And then, as if on cue, it began to rain. Without any warning, buckets of water fell from the sky, accompanied by a clap of thunder and a flash of lightning that turned the air yellow. The effect was so startling that everyone forgot what they were doing and started running for home. Jackets and equipment were left behind in the scramble, and Thomas almost forgot his backpack.

It rained so hard that the dried-out riverbed that ran alongside the property couldn't absorb any more moisture. The pounding water ate ridges into its slick surface, and a rushing stream started flowing along its path. The mud was so slippery it was difficult to stand, much less run, and Thomas's brand-new shirt and freshly ironed chinos got so saturated with water he could barely move his legs.

"Give me your hand," Thomas yelled as Violet stretched out an arm to him. "You're gonna fall if you don't hold on."

The dog circled the two children, barking furiously, keeping them together and trying to move them forward as if they were an errant flock of sheep. Violet lost her footing altogether and slid facedown into a deep and muddy furrow. Thomas tried to help her up and immediately got dragged down with her. The dog encouraged them to get up by barking and pushing them with his powerful head, and the two, drenched, tumbled forward.

Lewis was nowhere to be seen. The rain was coming down so heavily he could have been in front of their noses and they wouldn't have noticed him.

BEWARE OF DOG

And then it happened. Just as Thomas and Violet reached what they hoped was the sidewalk, a deafening crack resounded right above their heads. Within seconds, a bolt of lightning slammed into the elm tree that had towered over the little street for more than a hundred years. A shower of sparks flew from its upper branches, the whole tree shook, and a huge limb came crashing down.

"Look out!" Thomas shouted.

Without thinking, Thomas and Violet leaped out of its way and right into the street. They didn't see Mr. McCarthy's delivery truck heading directly toward them, and Mr. McCarthy didn't see the two friends. He was having a hard enough time keeping his truck from slipping off the road and wiping his foggy windshield with his sleeve.

It all happened so fast that when it was over no one could say exactly what had happened, but in a flash the dog had hurled his body at the children, sending them tumbling out of danger. The dog himself was not so lucky. In his attempt to save Thomas and Violet, he had been struck by the truck. Some instinct buried deep within had told him what to do, and he had listened.

And then, just as suddenly as the rain had started, it stopped. The air smelled like damp towels, and the sky turned a friendlier-looking shade of gray. Mr. McCarthy came rushing out of his truck to see if the children were all right. Thomas and Violet looked like scarecrows that had been left out in a tornado, but they were perfectly fine. Unaware of what had happened, they just wanted to find the dog.

"Here, boy. Here, boy. We're over here," Thomas shouted, and ran down the street and back toward the empty lot.

But the dog was nowhere to be seen. Violet searched the sidewalk, crossed the street more carefully this time, and hollered until she lost her voice. Their shaggy yellow friend was nowhere to be found.

Then Mr. McCarthy noticed a soggy tail emerging from under the left side of the truck. He told the children to cover their eyes as he got on his hands and knees and dragged out the poor animal.

"Is he okay?" Violet asked.

"I'm not looking, are you?" Thomas replied.

"Are you kidding?" she answered swiftly.

Although seriously injured, somehow the dog had managed to avoid being run over by the truck's massive wheels.

Mr. McCarthy eased a piece of plywood under the dog. He had been saving it in the back of the truck for a new sign he intended to make for Mostly McCarthy's, the little food shop he and his wife had recently established. He quickly covered the dog with a blanket he kept tucked under the front seat, and with the help of Thomas and Violet he loaded the animal into the back of the truck and sped away.

Thomas and Violet sat motionless. They were terrified to move, lest they disturb the noble animal resting on the makeshift stretcher they held across their laps.

A kindly old veterinarian, Doc Minderbinder, had an office about ten minutes away, and maybe, just maybe, there was something he could do to help.

CHAPTER THREE
Disaster

Even though they were going faster than they had any right to, to Thomas the truck seemed to be standing still. Violet reviewed the basic principles of CPR, which she had picked up from a show she watched on Direct-TV, but she couldn't remember whether they applied to dogs. With the injured dog on their laps, Thomas and Violet agreed that the only thing to do was to keep still in case the dog had a spinal injury and to stay alert in the event Mr. McCarthy issued any orders.

With every passing moment Thomas could

see the life draining out of the dog. His breathing was uneven and labored and occasionally appeared to stop altogether. But as they turned the corner onto Doc Minderbinder's street, Thomas heard a soft groaning sound emanating from beneath the blanket.

"He's still alive," Thomas said gratefully.

"Let's get this show on the road." Mr. McCarthy swerved into the driveway and was already out the door and on his way over to help with the dog.

"Steady, now. We've got to try and keep that dog immobile."

Together they started walking toward a cheerful red door, which was decorated with stenciled paw prints of various sizes and colors. They were careful to avoid a bed of geraniums planted in the shape of a giant bone. As they approached the entrance, they noticed an announcement stuck to the window: THROUGH THIS DOOR ENTER SOME OF THE

BEWARE OF DOG

MOST BELOVED CREATURES IN THE UNIVERSE — YOUR PETS.

Doc Minderbinder had a reputation for being the kindliest man in Cedar Springs, but as Thomas was not permitted even the tiniest of pets, he had never encountered the revered veterinarian. Several years ago he had sheltered an unusual species of ladybug in his dresser drawer, but the bug never got sick. And anyway, Thomas doubted that the welcome on Doc Minderbinder's door extended to the insect world.

Mr. McCarthy rang the doorbell, which produced a short series of computerized yips that sounded a lot like "Here Comes the Bride."

As they stood waiting, Mr. McCarthy turned solemnly to Thomas and Violet and said, "Doc Minderbinder is a wonderful vet. He cured two of my son's gerbils and removed a fur ball the size of Idaho from my cat's throat.

But he's not a magician. I want you two to remember that."

Thomas felt a lump forming in his throat and swallowed hard. The dog had saved his life, and he wasn't willing to entertain the possibility that someone couldn't save the dog's.

The door swung open, and a squat, obese woman stood before them. She was wearing a sailor hat embroidered with the words I'M NURSE LEONA, AND DON'T YOU FORGET IT perched jauntily on what appeared to be a completely bald head. Her tiny feet were encased in enormous white platform shoes that elevated her to just about eye level with Violet.

"Come in. Sit down," she said brusquely. "Leave the animal with me." She pointed to a gleaming silver gurney that smelled of alcohol and iodine. They placed the dog as carefully as they could onto the cart as the nurse twitched her huge round head in the direction of a cozy little waiting room off to one side. She handed Thomas a clipboard bulging with important-looking papers to fill out.

"Questions later, answers now," she barked.

Then, as if following orders from a suddenly remembered memo on appropriate nurse behavior, her stern features erupted into a huge grin. Instead of encouraging confidence, the gesture had a chilling effect. Thomas decided her skills probably lay outside the boundaries of public relations. Humming cheerfully, she briskly wheeled the dog through a swinging door, into the doctor's office.

So far the day had been filled with more adventure than Thomas had seen in his entire life. As he sat on a couch covered in faux dalmation fur, he caught his breath long enough to appreciate the irony of his current situation. For years he had imagined how much fun it would be to take his dog to the vet, and now that the moment had arrived, it wasn't fun at all. It was sad and scary and filled him with a hollow sense of dread.

Thomas and Violet tried to concentrate on back issues of *American Beagle* while Mr. McCarthy called his wife and told her to keep the bird in the oven. Suddenly, a tall, gaunt man dressed in black from head to toe emerged out of nowhere and addressed the three of them.

"Doc Minderbinder, at your service," he said in a high-pitched, nasal voice that bore a trace of a Middle European accent. "X rays will confirm my suspicions, but your pet appears to have been run over by a ten-ton truck."

Nurse Leona clucked in agreement as she scooped up Thomas's forms in her tiny round hands and quickly buried her face in them.

Doc Minderbinder grabbed the charts from her and pulled out a pair of ornate eyeglasses. Tiny twin microscopes protruded from their heavy metal frames. He held the papers about an inch away from his eyes as he eagerly manipulated the dials on the lenses with his long, tapering fingers.

"Interesting — very interesting." The doctor appeared utterly fascinated by Thomas's scribbles.

Thomas knew medical charts were important but couldn't understand why, in this case, they were receiving so much attention. Beyond writing down his name and address, he had left the dog's history entirely blank.

As quickly as he had entered the room, the doctor was gone. A thought buzzed noisily about in Thomas's head. It wasn't fully formed, but at its core there rested a kernel of skepticism. Why did the friendly doctor he had heard so much about remind him of Dracula?

Nurse Leona took a watering can from a shelf and began tending to pots of perfect-looking flowers lined up along the window-sills. Thomas quietly noted that the flowers were plastic and was about to give Violet a nudge when an alarmed cry echoed through-out the waiting room.

"Where's my scalpel? I want my scalpel!"

Nurse Leona stopped dead in her tracks, sending water from the can flying about in all directions.

"Hold your horses," she yelled as she flew into the inner sanctum to assist with the operation.

Thomas and Violet fidgeted nervously in their chairs. Nurse Leona came out after several tense minutes to give a progress report consisting primarily of glowing de-scriptions of Doc Minderbinder's prowess at the operating table.

"He has the forearms of a god," she claimed, and immediately whisked back into the inner office.

BEWARE OF DOG

All Thomas could think about was how the dog was doing. A little later, the doctor came out to say how well the operation was going. He referred to the "experimental nature" of some of the techniques he was employing to "get that puppy back on his feet and into the sandbox." Maybe that was the way all vets talked, but Thomas still thought he was a little odd.

Nurse Leona came out at last, and even though they begged to stay, at least until they were sure the dog would be okay, she insisted the children go home. While cautiously optimistic as to the outcome, Doc Minderbinder wanted them to know he would be working well into the night, and possibly the next day, too. He may be strange, Thomas thought, but he certainly is dedicated.

"Good evening, children," Nurse Leona intoned dryly as she handed them each a peppermint candy.

"Thank you, Nurse Leona," they responded in tandem.

Violet wasn't sure why, but something about Nurse Leona reminded her of the witch in "Hansel and Gretel."

It was eight o'clock by the time Mr. McCarthy deposited Thomas and Violet in front of their doorsteps and headed home for his seriously overcooked turkey dinner.

"Stop in at the store sometime, and we'll give you each a free bag of chips." Mr. McCarthy had received an extra shipment of barbecued potato chips that nobody seemed to want. He was having a special. Buy anything, get a free bag of chips.

Thomas hurried down the path to his front door. A few dark clouds still hovered overhead, and some errant drops of rain trickled down from trees and rooftops, but the storm had moved on. It would be a starry night.

Thomas opened the door as quietly as he

could, rehearsing a laundry list of excuses. He was two hours late for dinner and had neglected to call his parents. He wondered whether his mother would try the angry approach or the "I was so worried I called every hospital in town" version. To Thomas's surprise, the house was empty. Perhaps everybody was out scouring the neighborhood.

Thomas wandered into the kitchen. Sitting on the counter was a plate of delicious-looking fried chicken and corn on the cob, tightly covered in plastic wrap. A container of gravy sat nearby, next to a mound of freshly baked biscuits with a little sign that said EAT ME FIRST, I'M HOMEMADE. Thomas picked up a biscuit absentmindedly and started munching on it. He spotted a sign taped to the cabinet above the sink. WE'RE AT THE BIG GAME, WISH YOUR BROTHER LUCK. DON'T THROW YOUR CORNCOBS IN THE GARBAGE DISPOSAL. No one had even noticed that he was missing.

Thomas removed the plastic wrap from his lukewarm dinner, put it in his pocket to save for experiments, and took a couple of bites of the chicken. He didn't have much of an appetite. His mind was still on the dog.

He washed and dried his dishes, wiped away some crumbs that had fallen onto the counter, and went upstairs to get ready for bed. When he had brushed his teeth and laid out his clothes for the next morning, he got under the covers and stared at all of the dog pictures he had hanging on his wall.

He thought about Doc Minderbinder and wondered if the dog was still being operated on. He wondered if the dog would survive. He wondered if the dog would wake up in the middle of the night, lonely and afraid. He wondered if dogs could dream. He wondered if morning would ever come. And then he fell asleep.

CHAPTER FOUR
Transformations

Thomas was wide-awake and halfway out of bed before he looked at the clock on his dresser and realized it was four in the morning and still completely dark outside. He lay down and tried to go back to sleep. When that didn't happen, he went into his bathroom, lay on the cold tile floor, and reread a book on Pavlov's experiments with dogs.

This didn't exactly take his mind off Doc Minderbinder and the operation, but he did eventually fall back asleep. When he awoke, the lines from the tile were embedded in his cheek, and he could smell sausages and apple pancakes. Usually he looked forward to Sunday morning breakfast, but today all he could think about was if the dog had made it through the night.

Roger was still sound asleep, exhausted from winning the big game the night before. Thomas tiptoed quietly from the bathroom over to his closet, happy to let his brother doze the morning away. He dressed quickly and hurried downstairs.

Thomas peeked into the kitchen. His mother was at the counter, completely absorbed in removing every single lump from the pancake batter.

He had to get to Doc Minderbinder's office as soon as it opened. He thought about making a break for the front door but remembered his father hadn't yet gotten around to fixing its loud squeak. So instead he decided to try for the window next to the dining room.

He managed to open it without a sound, but just as his feet landed on the grass outside, his mother called out to him.

There was no reasonable explanation for his mother's uncanny ability to stop him every time he attempted to leave the house. His mother came equipped with an extremely developed form of something better than your average radar — motherly instinct.

As he made his way to the kitchen, back inside, Thomas tried to appear interested in the feast his mother had laid before him. He would have to finish at least a half dozen of the perfectly formed pancakes to avoid any more undue attention. Lack of appetite unleashed an anxiety in his mother that could ensure he would never get out of the house.

Mrs. Wiggins had just completed a seminar called "Breakfasts of the World, and How to Serve Them," and Thomas was relieved that today was the United States. Two days ago it was Sweden, and he had a tough time finding anything without fins or goat cheese. For Japan they all had to put on kimonos and eat on the floor.

Thomas wolfed down the pancakes and mushed around the rest of the food on his plate. He had to make it look like he had tasted a little of everything — a cardinal mealtime rule at the Wiggins's. Then Thomas started for the door. Barely looking up from her life-size needlepoint tapestry depicting Martha Stewart's career, his mother glanced at his plate and said, "Can't we do a little better than that?"

Thomas ate pancakes until he thought he might need hospitalization himself. At last he was able to make it out the door. He got on his bike and sped over to pick up Violet. He didn't even have to stop. She was waiting in front of her house, already perched proudly on her new red racing bike. As he whizzed by she caught up with him. She didn't have to ask where they were going. She had been up since five o'clock this morning, waiting for it to be late enough to go see Doc Minderbinder.

They rang the bell a couple of times, but the simulated yipping dog sound didn't attract any attention. So they started knocking, and when that didn't work, they started pounding. The door flew open, and Doc Minderbinder appeared so suddenly that Violet screamed.

The doctor didn't seem to notice. His bloodshot eyes darted about. His operating coat was torn and dirty, and his long black hair, which had been slicked back and parted precisely down the center yesterday, looked as if it had been attacked by an eggbeater. He was so tired he was supporting himself by leaning against the door frame. When he opened his mouth to speak, his voice came out in a hoarse whisper.

"Come back in an hour. I think he's going to make it." He closed the door in their hopeful faces.

To say that the hour passed slowly was putting it mildly. Thomas and Violet rode their bikes to the center of town and back seven or eight times, and still the minute hand on Violet's Xena Warrior Woman watch refused to complete its journey around the dial. They played Geography, a game neither one of them liked, for what they estimated to be at least twenty minutes but turned out to be three. As they completed their umpteenth round of Three-thirds of a Ghost, again the door flew open. The round woman spoke first.

"Say hello to *Mister I'm Better Now,* kids." Nurse Leona and Doc Minderbinder stood like proud parents beside a dazed and wobbly — but definitely standing — perfectly normal-looking dog. Or so it seemed.

BEWARE OF DOG

The sun shone and birds sang as the happy friends and one extremely groggy dog wended their way slowly toward Thomas's house. In his hand, Thomas clutched a handful of pamphlets on how to take care of your post-operative pet and a small plastic doctor's bag filled with doggie treats.

The dog was alive, and that was a wonderful thing. But Thomas couldn't imagine what in the world he was going to say to his parents. Granted, he would only attempt to keep the dog until his owner could be found, and not a second longer. And of course, the dog had nearly been killed, and he had saved both Thomas's and Violet's lives. Still, Thomas was not one hundred percent convinced the animal would be allowed into the house.

Nurse Leona had given them a thick piece of rope to attach to the dog's collar, in case he decided to bolt, but Thomas couldn't see why an animal who had recently risked his life to save theirs would want to run away. If he did, he certainly wouldn't get very far. The dog was still recovering from the effects of anesthesia and could barely walk in a straight line.

As the dog moved forward, his legs teetered precariously. Thomas had to keep preventing him from crashing into fire hydrants and trees. Just when he seemed to be getting the hang of forward motion, he slowed down, ground to a complete halt, and fell sound asleep, standing up.

Doc Minderbinder said that it would be a good idea to keep the dog moving. After an operation of this magnitude, he explained, it was important to make sure a patient didn't slip into a coma. While Thomas had never had any firsthand experience with comas, he wasn't planning on taking any chances. He gently prodded the sleeping dog, who opened his weary eyes, attempted to wag his tail, then fell over and promptly went back to sleep.

"This isn't good," Thomas said.

"Can't you do something?" asked Violet.

"Maybe."

Then Thomas unfolded a long list of special instructions Nurse Leona had tucked into the pamphlets. Way up near the top was a warning to keep the dog away from metal detectors. During the lengthy operation, a fair amount of the dog's insides had evidently been replaced with steel and aluminum. On the outside, fortunately, he still looked exactly like the rumpled golden retriever he had always been. In fact, in his haste to begin the operation, Doc Minderbinder had foregone the traditional cleansing of the patient. Thomas recognized yesterday's mud and leaves still clinging stubbornly to the dog's tangled fur.

It would be wise, the instructions continued,

to avoid letting the dog come in contact with electrical outlets of any kind. And most of all, never, never to allow him anywhere near a power plant.

Thomas thought about these and several other important caveats on the list as he and Violet tried waking the dog by shouting into his ears. When that didn't work, they tried hoisting the dog to his feet — a difficult task, as the operation had added at least ten or fifteen pounds to the dog's lean frame. But the dog kept falling over. Thomas wondered if this might indeed be the coma the doctor had warned them about. He tried shaking the dog while simultaneously hollering into his ears. Meanwhile, Violet wrapped the rope around her hand and tried in vain to pull the dog to his feet.

Officer Ericson, the friendly policeman who walked his beat in this sleepy part of town, looked over at them warily. "Easy on that dog, kids. We have laws about that sort of thing." He waited for them to stop before he walked off, whistling and swinging his club, satisfied he had done his job.

At that moment the little gray cat who lived in the neighborhood wandered over to see what the excitement was all about. Suddenly, an instinct stronger than the urge to sleep sent a shiver of excitement through the dog and seemed to will his exhausted body into action. He stood up, shook himself, and took off after the surprised feline. His speed was not even close to what he might have attained on a day he hadn't had major surgery, but he was fast enough to take Violet by surprise. She let go of the rope she was holding and watched, transfixed, as the chase began.

Thomas was the first to realize the danger that lurked on the other side of the block and down the street to the left. He jumped on his bike and raced away as fast as he could, but the light had turned red.

"Wait for me!" Violet cried. "I'm coming, too!"

The light turned green just as Violet caught up to Thomas, and off they raced.

Their feet pounded the pedals as they sped across the street, around the corner, and straight toward the power plant that provided all of the electricity for Cedar Springs and its tiny suburb, Wappinger's Falls.

Thomas jumped off his bike and ran toward the dog. He was watching the cat intently as it darted through a hole in the fence and escaped into the relative safety of the masses of coils that filled the center of the gigantic power facility.

The dog heard Thomas approaching and turned to look at him.

"Don't do it!" Thomas shouted at the top of

his lungs, and then he watched helplessly as the dog disregarded the advice and took off, somewhat shakily. The dog ran through the hole and deep into the canyons of electrical equipment. Violet caught up with Thomas and got off her bike, too.

"Where'd he go?" Violet asked, panting.

Thomas pointed glumly to a space between two extremely large and dangerous-looking coils.

"He wouldn't — he couldn't — he mustn't . . ." Violet couldn't bring herself to finish the thought.

Thomas could. "He did."

"Oh, no," she gasped.

Helpless, they both watched and waited for something terrible to happen.

It was quiet for a second, and Thomas was beginning to think Doc Minderbinder had been overly cautious in his warnings. Just then a smell like overheating metal, accompanied by loud barking and the crackling of millions of watts of surging electricity, sent Thomas's senses into overload.

He and Violet could only stare, openmouthed. Flashes of brilliant white light zigzagged around the circuits that crisscrossed through the miles of equipment, inside of which the two animals were currently trapped. The event was made all the more horrifying by the incongruously beautiful weather.

Officer Ericson heard the commotion and hurried over to see what was happening just as the singed cat hurtled back out of the hole in the fence, screeching hysterically. She ran madly down the street.

Officer Ericson looked at Thomas and Violet curiously. He had always thought of them as two of the town's most upstanding young citizens. When he saw what happened next, he made a note to schedule appointments with their parents.

A circle of electronic energy like a swirling, silvery-white tornado took shape around the perimeter of the electric coils and wound itself snakelike around the plant. Even with their eyes squeezed tightly shut, Thomas and Violet could sense the blinding fury of the current. Officer Ericson put on his sunglasses and shook his head.

The tornado whirled faster and faster as the electricity continued to pulse. Soon an intense humming sound filled the air. It was a strange kind of sound, but one that was not altogether unfamiliar to Thomas.

When he was in third grade, he and Violet had performed a series of experiments involving the principles of electromagnetism. If you multiplied it by a thousand, the little battery station they constructed made a sound exactly like the one he was hearing. The dog had wandered smack into the middle of what was becoming a magnetic field of astronomical proportions.

"Watch your head," Violet shouted.

Metal objects began flying, attracted by the field's enormous pull. Stray keys and coins and bottle caps went whizzing past. Thomas's gyroscope worked its way out of his pocket and headed straight for the swirling vortex. Officer Ericson's sunglasses and watch were next, followed by Violet's bicycle. She tried to hold onto it but quickly realized it was a losing battle. Thomas was desperately trying to hold onto his and was about to let go when a thunderous bang announced the end of whatever was happening.

A giant puff of ashy smoke rose mushroom-like from the center of what had been the tornado. Then the dog, much to everyone's surprise, shot straight up through the center of the smoke. Sailing out the top of the power plant about thirty feet into the air and over the fence, the dog landed squarely on all four paws, right at Thomas's feet.

After looking cautiously up at the sky and ascertaining that nothing else was dropping down, Thomas and Violet turned to look at the dog. He wagged his tail feebly and attempted a friendly bark. Except for the fact that every hair on his body was standing rigidly at attention at right angles to his skin, strangely enough he seemed perfectly fine. Officer Ericson had fainted on the spot.

CHAPTER FIVE
Welcome Home . . . Sort Of

Thomas got off his bike and gingerly guided the dog down the path to his front door. He had dropped Violet at her house first. She hated leaving Thomas and the dog for even a second.

"I don't want to miss any more excitement."

"Come for dessert. My mom's making s'mores," Thomas said.

Alicia would be coming over to baby-sit Thomas tonight, since Mr. and Mrs. Wiggins would be attending an all-city basketball awards dinner at which Roger was to be the guest of honor. He had managed to find some more records to break, and Mrs. Wiggins was already daydreaming about adding a small wing to the house for all the new trophies he would be bringing home. Roger told Thomas he found all the hoopla, as he liked to call it, pretty boring. If it was so boring, Thomas thought, then why did he get a haircut and buy new shoes and a dressy shirt to wear to the event?

Thomas wasn't exactly jealous, he explained to Violet, but it did make him just the slightest bit curious as to when he would ever truly distinguish himself at anything. It wasn't the prizes or the attention, he said, it was the satisfaction of knowing there was something you could do better than anybody else. Violet said she understood, but she didn't really. She knew that there were already plenty of things Thomas did better than anybody else.

Thomas had to move slowly as he led the dog home because the animal was still suffering from the effects of both the anesthesia and being jolted by a million volts of electricity. But he did seem to be a little steadier on his feet. Once or twice he even looked up at Thomas so gratefully that Thomas couldn't help but wonder what was going on behind his intelligent eyes. He believed more than ever before that dogs were a lot smarter than humans were willing to give them credit for.

Thomas had once read a book that explained that dogs could only experience time in the present tense and had no concept whatsoever of the future. Why, then, did they bury bones and come back for them days later for an afternoon snack? Thomas imagined there were lots of other things about dogs — especially this dog — that nobody really understood. If he could have taken even the smallest peek inside the mind of the perfectly ordinary-looking animal at his side, his suspicions would have been more than confirmed.

Something had happened to the dog this morning. Something extraordinary. The bits of metal the vet had used to put him back together had somehow reacted to the effects of the power surge and created a series of amazing changes. Thomas couldn't even imagine the magnitude of those changes. In fact, the molecules throughout the dog's body were still in the process of busily rearranging themselves. It would be several days before they had fully completed their magical transformation.

For one thing, the dog's previously all-black-and-white world was suddenly awash with greens and reds and yellows. Of course, being a dog and unable to express himself except by growling or barking, he could only stare in wonder at the amazing new world in which he suddenly found himself. A shiny purple car drove by, and it looked so delicious the dog could scarcely refrain from running after it and licking it.

A technicolor cat caught his attention, and the dog became so interested in the delicate orange-and-caramel markings that speckled the cat's body that it didn't even occur to the dog to chase her. This was fortunate, because the cat being observed with almost microscopic clarity was nearly two miles down the road.

When they reached the front door, Thomas searched for his house keys. He realized that they had been sucked through the fence that surrounded the power plant and had probably melted. He was glad that he and Violet had decided to take a solemn oath never to speak about the day's adventures to anybody. Officer Ericson was unlikely to carry tales. He had decided to go on immediate post-traumatic stress leave and would be spending the rest of the fall at his cousin's dude ranch in New Mexico.

Thomas made one last unsuccessful attempt to smooth down the dog's coat, which still stood stiffly and stubbornly at attention. The dog, he decided, bore a distinct resemblance to the Bride of Frankenstein.

And then a noise caught Thomas's attention. He immediately turned his head toward the street, because whatever it was seemed to be coming from that direction, but there was no one in sight. He looked down at the dog, and suddenly the noise stopped.

He listened more closely. He could hear the wind whistling and the distant buzzing of a leaf blower, but nothing that sounded precisely like the sound that still resonated inside his head. It was a quiet sound, and although it was unlike anything he had ever heard before, it wasn't unpleasant. It was almost as if someone was trying to talk to him without using words.

The more he tried to identify the image that was forming in his mind, the more elusive it became. He couldn't tell precisely what it was trying to say, but he had the distinct impression someone was desperately trying to tell him something.

At that exact moment the dog happened to be dreaming about the owner, the person he had come to think of as the smelly old lady. The woman was quite old and devoted to a powerful cologne called "Lilacs in May," with which she drenched herself regularly. The dog imagined her bending over to give him a treat, and then he thought about how wonderful it felt when her wrinkled and bony hands reached under his chin and scratched an especially annoying itch. A sudden and vivid memory of the old woman's flowery perfume made his nose practically shiver with excitement.

Thomas had no idea what was happening, but at that exact moment a picture of an old woman appeared inside his head. It was a little fuzzy, and Thomas simply dismissed it. But he couldn't help but wonder why he would be thinking about an old woman in a gray woolen dress he had never seen before in his entire life. And why did the sight of the stranger's gentle smile generate a glow of warmth and happiness somewhere deep inside of him?

The answer was as simple as it was unimaginable. The boy was somehow, un-explainably, able to read the dog's mind. As quickly as the old woman and the warm feeling had entered his consciousness, they faded. But he did wonder why, with autumn leaves falling everywhere and winter right around the corner, the scent of faded lilacs filled the air.

Suddenly, Thomas's father hurried out the front door. He was on his way to run the first errand on his long To Do list that Mrs. Wiggins taped neatly to the fridge every morning. As he stepped outside, he glanced down at his watch, tripped over the dog, and went flying into a well-manicured rosebush.

It wasn't the thorns. And it wasn't the scrape on his knee. It wasn't even the tear in his favorite jacket that caused him to shake and tremble. It was the proximity of what, to Mr. Wiggins, might as well have been a charging woolly mammoth. He started to call excitedly for help.

The poor dog, having no idea of the terror for which he was responsible, trotted over to the man and did his best to comfort him by jumping up and licking his face. Mr. Wiggins, adrenaline racing through his body, made the perfectly ridiculous assumption that the dog was attempting to eat him. He lost the ability to use words altogether and started leaping up and down and shrieking hysterically.

He turned red with embarrassment at his outcry but fought back tears of relief when Mrs. Wiggins came rushing out the door. She saw the boy and the dog, and she saw her husband trying frantically to hide himself behind the mangled rosebush. She grasped the situation immediately.

She instantly summoned everybody into the kitchen for a family conference. The dog remained outside, safely tethered to a section of metal grillwork that decorated the side of the house.

CHAPTER SIX
Where'd He Go?

Mr. Wiggins attended the family meeting from high atop a kitchen stool. He was ready to leap to the safety of a nearby countertop in the event the dog managed to pull loose from his moorings and attack the kitchen. Roger was positioned strategically by his father's side with instructions to tackle the dog if necessary.

All in all, Thomas thought, it hadn't gone too badly. Mrs. Wiggins simply reminded Thomas that if the dog shed, or drooled, or knocked over anything, or ventured within twenty feet of Mr. Wiggins, she was very sorry, but hero or not, he would have to be put into a kennel until his owner could be found. Assuming the dog was able to meet these stringent criteria, he would be allowed to stay in Thomas's room for a period of up to thirty-six hours, and not a second longer.

The family meeting ended abruptly when Mr. Wiggins suddenly remembered that even though it was Sunday, he had a large amount of catch-up work to complete at the office and rushed off. Nobody believed him. He was, of course, too frightened to remain at home with a dog in the house.

Roger hurried to Alicia's for a history study date, and Mrs. Wiggins had to make an emergency visit to the mall.

Thomas was relieved to find himself alone in the house at last. He waited until his parents' car was well out of the driveway and down the block before eagerly venturing into the yard to welcome the dog into his new home. He was shocked to find that not only was the dog nowhere in sight, but the section of the wall to which the dog had been tied was missing as well. A jagged hole the size of a large piano revealed a section of Mrs. Wiggins's perfectly decorated living room.

How far, Thomas wondered, could a dog with a large metal grate and a four-foot section of wall attached to his leash get? In the case of this particular dog, the answer was very far. Thomas followed a deep furrow of destroyed lawn down to the sidewalk and continued along a trail of dirt and flowers toward Violet's house. What exactly, he wondered, was going on?

Perhaps the section of the house to which the dog was attached had fallen into disrepair due to some kind of intense termite activity. It was unlikely such a thing could ever occur under his mother's watchful eye, but it did fall within the realm of possibility. Maybe it had simply fallen apart under the dog's insistent tugging.

It was certainly more believable than the truth. How could Thomas have realized that the dog possessed the strength of ten dogs, and his abilities were multiplying with every second? In another few hours he would be able to move not just a section of the wall but the entire house as well, if he wanted to.

Thomas knocked on Violet's door. Mrs. Schnayerson opened it.

"Hi, Thomas, would you like to come in for milk and cookies?"

"No thanks, Mrs. Schnayerson."

Penny Schnayerson gave her daughter a holler, and Violet and Thomas dashed out the door.

"Maybe this is all just a dream," Violet said as she and Thomas raced around the neighborhood, searching high and low for the missing dog. "A terrifying dream," she continued. "Maybe we've stumbled through a hole in time, and we're living in an alternate reality."

Thomas didn't even take the time to reply. He had to find the dog, clean up the lawn, and repair the damage to the house before his parents got home. He didn't have much use for speculation. Plain old regular reality, in this case, was frightening enough.

And then Violet spotted the dog. He was perched way at the top of a very tall tree, looking as if this were the most normal place in the world for a dog to find himself. The side of Thomas's house was still attached to his leash and dangled down through the branches.

A stunned cat was cowering at the tip of the most distant branch she could find. The poor animal was still lightly toasted around the edges from her run-in with the dog at the power plant. For a second it occurred to

Thomas that maybe Violet was right. This didn't resemble any reality he had ever seen.

The dog had chased after the cat, unaware that he was dragging about four hundred pounds of extra baggage along for the ride. His urge to chase was so powerful that he didn't even notice the piece of wall ripping away from the house. The frantic cat reached the tree, leaping to what she thought was safety. Then she climbed to a high branch, only to have the dog follow her effortlessly up the side of the tree.

If Thomas could have been there to watch, he would have been amazed at the ease with which the dog was able to grip onto the slippery trunk, using his teeth, claws, and brute strength. He pulled himself and the piece of house more than thirty feet into the air without a second's hesitation.

"Bad dog." The words were scarcely out of Thomas's mouth before the dog wheeled around, twisted his head downward, and peered through the branches. He seemed to be thinking, What have I done? I'm a good dog. In fact, that's exactly what he was thinking. Thomas had taken another unknowing peek directly into the mind of the animal.

If he could have seen inside the dog's head, Thomas would have been astonished. The cells inside the dog's brain were still busily multiplying and diversifying. Already his IQ had expanded to well beyond that of even the most brilliant porpoise, and his transformation was still far from complete. He was about to become the most intelligent four-legged animal in the universe. But right now all he wanted was for the boy with the stern expression on his face to forgive him and pat him on the head.

The cat took this opportunity to make a flying leap onto the roof of a nearby house.

BEWARE OF DOG

The dog tried to follow, dropping down abruptly from the tree like a giant stone. He landed with a dull thud directly in front of Thomas. The chunk of house hit next and smashed into a million tiny pieces. Only the grate, solid metal through and through, remained intact. The dog looked sheepishly up at Thomas.

"Now you've really done it," Thomas said, shaking his head. Thomas had no idea how important it was to the dog to make a good impression on him or he wouldn't have said anything. The dog looked crestfallen.

In fact, until the arrival of the cat, the dog had spent several minutes with his ear glued to the wall, listening to Mrs. Wiggins's speech. He didn't understand the words, but he could tell from her tone of voice that he had better avoid doing bad things if he wanted to keep a roof over his head. The precise nature of those things was something of a mystery to him, but he had every intention of being very, very good indeed.

Realizing the enormity of whatever he must have done to cause such disapproval, he made a mad dash back to the house. Thomas and Violet did their best to keep up. When the dog arrived, he noticed the hole in the side of the wall and tried unsuccessfully to push the grate into the space where the missing wall had stood. Then he took his place in front of it and tried to pretend that nothing was the slightest bit amiss.

"Stay," Thomas commanded. And much to Violet's surprise, that is exactly what the dog did.

For the next two hours Thomas and Violet pushed and prodded every last piece of sod and grass and flower back into a semblance of the perfect lawn Mrs. Wiggins cherished. The fact that the sun was beginning to set gave Thomas some hope that when his family returned to change for the big dinner, no one would notice the havoc that had been wreaked on that lovely stretch of velvetlike green lawn.

There was, however, absolutely nothing that either Thomas or Violet could think of to do to restore the missing piece of the house. They considered taping a large sheet of paper over the gaping hole but decided that would make it even more noticeable.

When they finally spied Mrs. Wiggins jogging casually back from the mall, carrying a large box filled with supplies, the two of them took their cues from the dog and pretended they didn't notice anything had happened, either.

As Mrs. Wiggins started up the walk, Mr. Wiggins pulled into the driveway. She looked up from the box, saw the hole in the wall, and exclaimed over and over, "Oh, my!" The dog immediately put his tail between his legs, closed his eyes tightly, and began a low whimper.

Mr. Wiggins got out of his car and started walking toward the house, careful not to go anywhere near the dog. He was transfixed by the sight of his perfect living room peeking out at him through the giant hole. He was about to say something when Mrs. Wiggins ran over to him, started to cry, and threw herself into his arms.

Thomas sighed deeply. The dog hadn't even made it into the house, and already he was to be banished. And then he heard his mother's voice. It was hard to understand at first. She was gasping for breath and making little crying noises in between the words, but Thomas could make out a couple of them, and they didn't sound so bad.

"Honey," sigh, gulp, sob, "I love my

anniversary," sob, sob, "surprise," gulp, sigh. "You're soooo thoughtful."

As they walked arm in arm into the house, Mr. Wiggins decided to keep his mouth shut, as he had completely forgotten that today was his seventeenth wedding anniversary. Somehow his wife thought the hole in the wall was a gift. Mrs. Wiggins dabbed the tears from her eyes with an embroidered handkerchief she kept for just such occasions.

"Beginning construction on the new trophy wing, all on your own," she said, gasping, "is about the sweetest thing you have ever done for me."

If this wasn't an alternate reality, Violet thought, it certainly was a strange one.

CHAPTER SEVEN
Food, Glorious Food

Alicia arrived on time. Mrs. Wiggins was relieved. She needed to prepare the table and set up the decorations before the rest of the parents arrived at the awards dinner, and she didn't want to be late.

"There's a pie in the oven, ice cream's in the freezer, and if anybody wants it, there's an angel food cake in the pantry," she said. "Oh, and make sure everybody drinks plenty of milk. Nobody ever drinks enough milk."

Alicia pretended to listen attentively and

made a mental note to arrive on an empty stomach next time she baby-sat.

Mrs. Wiggins handed the baby-sitter a list of printed instructions for the evening, ranging from room-cleaning particulars for Thomas to a time-flow management chart of the night's activities: 6 P.M., eat; 7 P.M., floss and brush; 7:30 P.M., begin homework, etc., etc.

Even Thomas's favorite allowable snack foods were listed in order of preference, with a reminder that additional flossing and brushing might become necessary. Alicia was an experienced baby-sitter, but she had never run across a mother quite like Mrs. Wiggins.

As soon as Roger and his parents were out the door, she hurled herself onto the living room sofa, grabbed a bag of potato chips, and turned on the television set. Thomas and Violet ran upstairs to see what the dog was up to.

"Don't kill each other," Alicia yelled after them, and turned up the volume.

Thomas took quick inventory of the room. He was tremendously relieved to find no apparent signs of mass destruction. The dog looked up at him, started to wag his tail excitedly, and almost let loose with an ecstatic hello bark. He immediately realized that loud noises were probably on his lengthy Don't List and stopped himself midbark. Instead the dog resumed staring at the wall, trying not to move, two activities he felt certain were on his rather short Do List. With all his heart, he wanted to be good.

"What would you like to eat, fella?" asked Thomas, petting the dog's head. All of a sudden a picture of a thick, juicy steak, medium rare and smothered in onions, popped into Thomas's head. The image was so realistic his mouth started to water. He could practically smell sizzling fat. Why, he wondered, was he thinking of a steak dinner when he wasn't the least bit hungry? And why did a huge container of vanilla ice cream suddenly appear on top of the image of the steak?

The dog looked at him longingly and whimpered. He hadn't had a decent meal since he began his adventure and was about to faint from hunger. Steak and vanilla ice cream were his favorite foods.

"Guess we're gonna have to do some shopping," said Thomas. The dog was so relieved he practically started to weep. "How'd you feel about a nice juicy steak?" The dog could control himself no longer. He became so excited he jumped onto Thomas's lap and yelped so loudly that Alicia tore herself loose from the program she was watching, ran up the stairs, and poked her head in the door.

"Is that dog hurting somebody?" she

asked, glancing at the three of them suspiciously.

The dog immediately sat down and tried to look as harmless as possible. Violet jumped in.

"I was practicing roller-skating and rolled over one of his paws, but I don't think it's broken."

As if he understood perfectly, the dog started to lick his paw and whimpered.

Violet gave Thomas a look that seemed to ask what in the world was going on. Fortunately, Alicia failed to notice there wasn't a roller skate in sight and hurried back downstairs to watch a particularly captivating rerun of *Dawson's Creek*.

The smelly old lady had completely spoiled the dog, feeding him the finest home-cooked meals. After steak and vanilla ice cream, his favorite items were anything from McDonald's to chicken Kiev.

Thomas and Violet tiptoed downstairs. The

dog tiptoed after them. As the dog ran to get the rope leash Nurse Leona had provided, he felt a little pang of sadness. He had grown to love the well-worn antique leather leash and collar the smelly old lady had used whenever they went for walks in the park together. Thomas wasn't sure why, but he, too, felt a little pang of sadness when he saw the dog standing there with the makeshift leash. He made a mental note to stop at the pet store on his way home from school tomorrow and purchase a proper one.

As they sneaked past the den, Alicia sat on the couch, hypnotized in front of the flickering TV.

If they hurried, they could do some shopping at Mostly McCarthy's before it closed. Then they could make dinner for the dog, and clean the dishes before Thomas's family returned from their event. Thomas didn't really expect the dog to understand, but as they made their way to the door he explained that this evening's meal was going to be a special treat. A welcome to the house sort of thing, not to be expected on a regular basis.

The dog understood exactly what Thomas was getting at and shot back an instant nonverbal but highly effective reply. He performed a certain noisy bodily function that, as Thomas's mother would frequently remind the family, belonged only in the bathroom and was to be accompanied by a heavy dose of air freshener. To put it bluntly, the dog passed wind.

Thomas shot a nasty look at Violet, who issued a vehement denial and shot the look right back at Thomas. Then they both looked at the dog, who tried to look as indignant as possible and then, in a tacit admission of guilt, tried to hide under the rug.

There was no way a full-grown golden retriever could possibly get under a two-by-three-foot throw rug. The dog managed to successfully cover only his large head and a small portion of his torso. The rest of his gangly body lay exposed for all to see, sprawled out on the floor.

A giant laugh bubbled up inside Thomas. It began somewhere near his toes and worked its way quickly up the rest of him. As he tried desperately to suppress it, it emerged as a giant series of snorts. Violet caught an enormous case of the giggles, and Alicia finally noticed something was going on. The three of them had been caught sneaking out of the house.

"Bring back Fritos," Alicia said, and turned right back to her beloved program.

Shopping was uneventful, although Thomas wasn't sure why every time he tried to buy a more inexpensive brand, he felt an over-whelming urge to purchase only Häagen-Dazs ice cream. The dog had a wonderful time sniffing and exploring.

The shoppers quickly returned home. The meal was cooked, and the dog ate voraciously. Alicia fell asleep the minute the rerun of *Dawson's Creek* was over. Violet wasn't surprised. Her sister never slept at night. She e-mailed friends around the world, gave herself French manicures, and practiced creating new hairstyles to attract Roger.

Upstairs once more, Violet helped Thomas rearrange his room.

"Your mom's not gonna be happy about this," Violet warned.

"I'll just put everything back in the morning," Thomas said confidently. But he knew Violet was right.

Together, they pushed his bed into the corner to make room for a couple of old cushions they found in the basement. They were careful not to disturb Roger's area. Even though the collection of ribbons and jerseys appeared haphazard and randomly displayed, Thomas's brother knew the precise location of every single one.

The dog walked over to his new sleeping area, sniffed the cushions cautiously, and practiced lying down on them a couple of times. He seemed satisfied, made a couple of circles around the makeshift bed, and then curled up on it to rest. His mouth opened wide in a huge yawn, and he closed his eyes.

The dog had been a tiny puppy when the kindly old woman came upon him at Kmart. His original owners had been suddenly called out of town and had reluctantly left the dog in the parking lot with a large sign around his neck that read, I'M GENTLE. I'M HOUSEBROKEN. TAKE ME HOME. Without a second's hesitation the old woman took the frightened little dog home. She was known throughout the area for her enormous and varied collection of stray animals. They all lived, in varying degrees of harmony, in her living room.

Always dependable and a natural organizer, the dog became the woman's right-hand animal. Using his teeth, nose, and paws, he helped feed the other animals. He also made sure that none of them strayed too far or ran into the street.

The dog even baby-sat for the chickens when they left their nests to get a drink of water or go for a walk around the back hallway. Although the dog found the chore somewhat embarrassing, he was extremely delicate with the eggs when he sat on them. He was patient and gentle with the chicks when they finally hatched, and several of them actually came to prefer the dog to their natural mothers. With a veritable Noah's ark camped in her living room, the old woman took to wearing a distinctive, rather pungent, lilac perfume wherever she went. The dog's days were spent eating her delicious meals and playing Frisbee with her. And even though the woman couldn't throw very well or very far, the dog loved chasing after the moving saucer.

The dog thought about the life he had left behind, and then he thought about how lucky he had been to find Thomas. Up to now, he had never spent a night away from home, and the presence of his new friend did a lot to alleviate the loneliness he was experiencing.

He opened a sleepy eye for a moment, gazed over at the pictures of the dogs on the wall, and wished they would go away.

At that exact moment, Thomas got up on a chair and patiently removed every one of them. He handed each poodle and weimaraner carefully down to Violet, who put them in his top drawer.

"Guess we won't be needing these for a while, will we?" he murmured.

Violet hoped Thomas wasn't becoming too attached to the dog. After all, he would only be staying for a little while.

"You know, you've never really liked golden retrievers all that much," she ventured.

The dog's ears perked up, and he appeared somewhat agitated.

"Quiet, Violet. He'll hear you."

"Yeah, right," Violet replied, and decided she'd better get back to her house.

Thomas's parents would be returning soon.

Before Violet left, she and Thomas made a plan to hunt for the dog's owner the next day after school. They would pretend they were preparing for the science fair and steal a couple of hours of searching time.

And then it was bedtime, and Thomas's parents came home and paid Alicia, who managed to remain awake for a couple of minutes. She had cleaned the living room only seconds before their arrival and made sure Thomas was in his pajamas and ready for bed. They thanked her profusely.

Usually it was Mr. Wiggins who performed the nighttime rituals. He would turn out the lights and tell Thomas a funny story about work.

"For a while," his mother explained, "I'll be putting you to bed at night. Dad has a very important project he's got to finish, and we're all going to have to pull together. We will have to pretend," she continued, "that we are the family from *Little House on the Prairie,* sacrificing individual needs for the greater good of the home."

No, Thomas thought, they would have to pretend their father wasn't locked in his bedroom, trying to avoid possible contact with the monster that was resting so contentedly on the pile of pillows on the floor.

As soon as she left the room, the dog opened a sleepy eye, got out of his bed, and hopped up onto Thomas's. He wasn't planning on sleeping on a bunch of pillows on the floor when there was a cozy bed with Thomas in it right in front of his nose.

Thomas immediately reached over and put an arm around the dog, who settled down next to him. The dog lay his head on the pillow right beside Thomas's. There they remained, eye to eye, nose to nose. The dog seemed to be memorizing Thomas's face. At last Thomas spoke.

"Don't worry, we'll find your real home."

He tried to sound confident, but he wasn't, really.

He certainly didn't expect a response. But he got one. He heard a little voice reply, and Thomas almost jumped out of his pajamas. He looked around the room and made sure he had turned off his radio and his CD player. He had. Was the portable TV that sat on the edge of his desk still on? It wasn't.

And then he looked right into the dog's

eyes, and he knew immediately. Thomas wasn't sure why, but he felt absolutely certain that the dog was trying to let him know he was very, very grateful.

"You're a good dog," Thomas said, and pulled the covers right up to both of their chins and lay back and stared at the ceiling. He was so happy he could barely stand it. He doubted he would ever fall asleep, and he didn't care. And then he sensed the voice again. The dog was desperate. Thomas suddenly had a picture in his head of a very large vanilla ice cream cone.

Thomas issued the dog a firm but gentle no. A moment later he detected the telltale odor of the dog's defiant gesture rising from beneath the sheets, accompanied by a sound like air escaping from a balloon. He was a wonderful dog, but he wasn't necessarily a good dog.

CHAPTER EIGHT
Evil Arrives

Both Thomas and the dog slept fitfully. The dog had a series of dreams about the smelly old lady. In one of them she was being rushed to the hospital. There was an ambulance and a loud siren. The noise frightened the dog. The dog sat next to the woman and knew she was in trouble, only nobody would tell him what the trouble was.

And then he dreamed that he fell from a great height and rolled down a hill, which, indeed, he had. He twisted and turned and hogged the covers. When he crash-landed at the bottom of the hill he sat up and barked. Thomas woke up immediately, hugged the dog tightly, hoped his parents hadn't heard the noise, and fell back to sleep.

Thomas had dreamed about the things he usually dreamed about. He discovered a secret passageway in his basement that led to an abandoned room that contained an ancient pharaoh's treasures, complete with a living, breathing Egyptian temple dog. And then he found himself in a large stadium. He and the dog were running in a race. Thousands of viewers cheered them on as they crossed the finish line a whisker ahead of their nearest competitor, who looked a lot like Lewis Musser.

As the dream continued, an ambulance drove by and Thomas jumped in, leaving the dog behind. An old lady was inside, and there was another dog next to her, a golden retriever. A loud siren wailed and a red light flashed and something terrible was happening, but no one would tell him what it was. The woman wasn't anyone he knew, but she seemed familiar. She smelled like flowers, and she was in trouble.

The next thing Thomas knew, he and the dog were tumbling down a gigantic hill. They landed with a crash, and Thomas woke up. What an unusual dream, he thought as he comforted the frightened animal, who seemed to have awoken from an equally disturbing nightmare.

Twice more that night the dog barked and sat up, and each time Thomas awoke at the same moment. Then he would do his best to comfort the dog and try to go back to sleep. By the time morning rolled around, Thomas and the dog were lying together, exhausted, in a heap at the bottom of the bed.

School days usually began with his mother poking her head into Thomas's room and singing a couple of bars of "Oh, What a Beautiful Morning." Today she made it through the entire song and even added a number of pokes and shakes before Thomas got up and headed groggily for the bathroom. The dog snored peacefully and never even opened his eyes.

As Thomas's mother put the finishing touches on a Hawaiian luau breakfast, Thomas got dressed, straightened up his room, and woke the dog by yelling "vanilla ice cream" into his ear.

While the dog stretched and sniffed around his new quarters, Thomas ran a lint brush over his bed and picked up a significant mound of dog hair. "If we don't do something about your fur, you won't last a day."

By the time Thomas went downstairs, the dog was covered from stem to stern in a series of hair nets held together by rubber bands. He wore a shower cap over his head for extra protection and Ziploc bags on his paws. No stray hair could possibly escape this humiliating outfit. The dog stood awkwardly in the middle of Thomas's room as if he were getting ready to perform an operation under the most sterile conditions.

After breakfast Thomas sneaked back upstairs. He brought a bowl of water and a couple of slices of pineapple French toast dipped in coconut and chopped macadamia nuts.

As Thomas stood holding the tray of food, he said, "You've got to be really good today. No barking. And you can't leave this room — not even for a second. You understand?" he asked, looking deep into the dog's eyes. The dog moaned and whined, but Thomas refused to set the food down until he finally sensed the dog had understood him. He failed to notice that the dog was keeping his rear paws discreetly crossed.

BEWARE OF DOG

"I'll be back in a couple of hours to walk you. Be good!" he said as he patted the dog's head and hurried off to school.

Thomas met Violet on the corner as usual, and they ran to catch the bus that would bring them to Stevenson School. They sat huddled together as far in the back as they could get. Thomas could hardly wait to tell her that he and the dog had established some sort of psychic connection. First he made Violet promise, on the life of her sister, never to reveal the secret to anyone.

"Maybe we could all appear on *Ripley's Believe It or Not!*," Violet said, her eyes widening.

And then Steven Winkleman, a third-grader with enormous feet, got on the bus. He clomped over and sat down right next to them, putting a stop to all conversation. He was all worked up because he had just completed a five-page book report, single-spaced, and couldn't wait to tell everybody. Thomas and Violet congratulated him and gave each other a little smile that said, "If you only knew *our* exciting news."

The yellow bus wound its way around the sleepy town while the dog sat uneasily in Thomas's room looking out the window. He felt a profound sense of embarrassment at the outfit Thomas had assembled for him. He had decided against ripping the hair nets off and was glad he hadn't when the mother stopped in to check on him before leaving for stenciling class. She expressed visible relief to see him wearing Thomas's wonderful no-shed solution.

Alone again, the dog stared out the window until the cat — barely recovered from the attack of the dog-with-the-house-attached-to-his-leash—sauntered by. The dog looked down and started barking ferociously. The cat, feeling herself at a safe distance, stopped beneath the window, looked up at the dog, and hissed tauntingly.

The dog knew he was being taunted and tried desperately to squelch the emotions that were coursing through his veins. Then the cat lay down and tormented the dog further by rolling over lazily and peering calmly up at the window.

The dog had an idea. He had been told to stay in his room. No one said anything about not throwing things out the window. He looked around, spotted a large plaster of paris model of the solar system sitting on the desk, maneuvered it onto the window ledge, and before the cat had a chance to notice what was happening, launched it straight down, where it landed squarely on the cat's tail.

The cat let out a howl and looked up at the window in disbelief. She had occasionally been chased and frequently barked at, but no dog had ever thrown anything at her before.

The cat flew down the street and almost got run over by a little boy on a tricycle. The dog's true nature could be contained no longer. He might be the strongest and he might be the fastest living thing in the world, but he was still a canine. He forgot his promise to be good. He didn't even think about possible eviction from his safe haven. A cat was running, and the dog needed to be chasing — and that was that.

The little boy almost fell off his tricycle when he saw the dog in the hair nets and shower cap and Ziploc booties leap out of the second-story window and run after the cat.

The dog landed smoothly, on all four paws. He was getting used to making landings from great heights by now. He chased the fleeing animal, leaping over cars and trees in frantic pursuit of the annoying cat.

Except for the little boy there were only two other passersby. The dog was too distracted to notice the odd-looking tall, gaunt man in a black overcoat and the tiny fat woman wearing high-heeled rain boots, a slicker, and a matching cowboy hat covered with question marks.

Rumors about the incident at the power plant had reached them, and Nurse Leona and Doc Minderbinder had taken advantage of the beautiful sunny day to stroll on over and satisfy their curiosity. If Thomas had been there, he might have wondered what the busiest vet in town and his nurse were doing out of the office at nine o'clock in the morning. He might also have wondered why they were both peering over the tops of newspapers, excitedly watching the dog with the speed of a cheetah race by.

The dog was moving so quickly that he created a gust of wind in his wake that almost took off the woman's hat. If Thomas had been there he might also have noticed that their newspapers were upside down. They weren't reading at all. They were spying on the dog.

As they continued to watch, the dog overtook the cat and wiggled out of his hair net bodysuit. He managed to swing it around with his teeth, throw it into the air, and lasso the frightened animal with uncanny accuracy. The cat fainted. The dog threw the motionless, netted animal over his shoulder and ran off to show Thomas how well he had done.

"Interesting quadruped, *n'est-ce pas*?" Nurse Leona batted her long false eyelashes at the doctor and chuckled drolly. As she laughed, a little piece of spinach that had been lodged in one of her front teeth flew out of her mouth and landed on the doctor's overcoat. She attempted to wipe it off by making a sudden and, she hoped, charming little gesture with her left hand, and managed to hit the doctor in the face. She uttered the only other French phrase she knew, which was *"oo-la-la."*

The doctor didn't look amused. All he could think about was the dog. And how much he needed him. And how much he wanted him. He determined then and there that he didn't care how, and he didn't care when, but he was going to get that dog back if it was the last thing he did.

The doctor had a plan. An evil one and a secret one. A dog with superpowers was just what he needed to execute it.

The dog caught up to the school bus, which had just arrived at Stevenson School and was dropping off the students. He was so happy to see Thomas and Violet that he took a running hop, skip, and jump and leaped on top of the bus.

Thomas circled around to the side, and when no one was looking, he waved at the dog and said, "Let the cat go." Thomas tried to sound as stern as possible, but the dog acted as if he had no idea what Thomas was trying to say. The cat had come to and was trying with all her might to claw and bite her way out of the netting.

"Bring me the cat!" shouted Thomas.

Thomas was positive the dog understood his command, but still the dog made no move to let go of the poor animal. Thomas shinnied awkwardly up the side of the bus and found himself face-to-face with the dog, who pretended he thought Thomas had climbed all the way to the top of the bus just to play with him.

The dog snagged a pine cone from a low-hanging branch, ran over to Thomas, and dropped it at his feet. He jumped around eagerly, as if he thought Thomas might throw the pine cone and engage him in a game of fetch.

"Bad dog," said Thomas sternly.

BEWARE OF DOG

The words didn't have their desired effect this time. The dog took a flying leap off the bus, the cat still slung over his shoulder, and started running down the street. He wasn't letting go of his prize so easily. As loud as he could, Thomas yelled the two words he thought might have an effect on the animal.

"NO DINNER."

The dog stopped in his tracks so quickly, sparks flew. The cat was catapulted out of the net and ran for her life. The dog hurried obediently back to the bus and tried unsuccessfully to scramble back into his hair nets and shower cap.

"Good dog," said Thomas, giving the dog a forgiving pat. Then Thomas raced off to attend his first class. He was already several minutes late, but he didn't care. He had a dog. At least for the day.

That day, every time he worked out a difficult

math problem, or got bossed around by Lewis Musser, or presented a complicated social studies report, he would see his friend pressing his big tan nose up against the window and leaving a big wet smudge, and nothing else would matter. At last the final bell rang, and Thomas and Violet and the dog headed for home.

When they passed a McDonald's, the dog went crazy. He started hopping around and whining and begging to go into the restaurant.

Violet decided to try reasoning with the dog. "We can't always get what we want, you know."

The dog looked at her warily.

Undaunted, she continued. "Let's go home and have some yummy dog food." The animal couldn't believe his ears. He simply threw himself onto the ground in front of Thomas and began to howl pitifully.

BEWARE OF DOG

"Nice try," Thomas said. Several people stopped to see if Thomas was beating the dog, which was exactly what the dog had intended.

A couple of minutes later, two children and a satisfied dog with a very greasy face and whiskers headed toward Thomas's house. The dog tried to make up for his bad behavior. He stayed close to Thomas and never once chased a bird or a squirrel. Thomas was beginning to realize, however, that when it came to either cats or food, the dog was simply and absolutely out of control.

"I might as well name you McGrowl," Thomas said. "At least you'll come when I call you." The dog realized Thomas had decided to name him after his favorite restaurant, which McGrowl thought was perfectly wonderful.

"Here, McGrowl," Thomas called, and the dog perked up his ears and ran to him.

Except for the fact that the dog still had no idea if he would ever see the smelly old lady again, he was having a terrific time.

When they arrived home, Nurse Leona and Doc Minderbinder were standing smack in front of Thomas's doorstep. Nurse Leona tapped her tiny foot impatiently. She carried a leash that was made of metal links. It looked like it weighed ten pounds.

"Good news, big boy," said the oversized nurse with a sly grin on her face. "We're taking you home." Thomas looked around. It took him a moment to realize that she was referring to McGrowl. She started to make a strange series of vaguely musical sounds. She couldn't carry much of a tune, but Thomas thought he recognized a couple of mangled bars of "My Favorite Things," from *The Sound of Music.* She attached the leash to McGrowl's collar and started walking the reluctant animal back down the driveway.

BEWARE OF DOG

Doc Minderbinder leaned down to whisper confidentially to Thomas, and both children recoiled. His breath smelled like formaldehyde.

"We've managed to locate the dog's rightful owners," he said, nearly bowling them both over. "Isn't that wonderful?"

Thomas didn't say a word.

"Little Susie and Cicely are sitting in my office even as we speak," he continued. "Such sweet sisters."

The doctor's voice sounded remarkably like a snake hissing. Thomas didn't think the doctor's news sounded so wonderful.

Looking mockingly at Thomas and Violet, he said, "Many thanks for returning the dog in the condition in which you found him. I am most grateful."

The doctor gave a little bow and then practically danced down the driveway as he caught up with Nurse Leona and the dog. The odd-looking couple did a little jig as they turned onto the sidewalk, dragging McGrowl along with them. McGrowl turned to look back at the children, with an expression that seemed to beg for help. Nurse Leona just hummed louder and pulled more tightly at the leash, forcing the dog back into a heel position.

McGrowl was in danger. Clearly, Doc Minderbinder and his nurse were not the kindly people they pretended to be. Clearly, Thomas had to do something about it.

CHAPTER NINE
Working on the Chain Gang

McGrowl's desperate plea for help still lingered in Thomas's mind. He was determined to pay a visit to Minderbinder's tonight, before something awful befell his new furry friend.

"What d'you think they're up to?" Violet queried.

"Don't think about it," Thomas replied tersely.

Violet continued, undaunted. "I heard once about a ring of thieves who stole dogs and made fur coats out of them." She frequently got her news from the *National Enquirer.* Fortunately, most of the facts she gathered there were completely unfounded.

"I can't imagine that's what's happening to McGrowl."

"Imagine it," she replied dramatically.

Thomas and Violet spent a couple of minutes messing up Mrs. Wiggins's kitchen so that she would think they were getting ready to start work on their science project. They pulled out several drawers and sprinkled around a number of the small paper cups she used for baking mini-soufflés.

Thomas's mother finally came in to see what they were up to. She gasped when she found them opening cans of her favorite imported water chestnuts and throwing away the contents. They explained they would be using the empty containers as beakers. When she heard they were on their way to Violet's house to complete the project, she was so relieved she didn't even ask where McGrowl was.

Thomas told his mother not to expect him home in time for dinner. He said that forty percent of their science grade would be determined by this project, and he and Violet might be working well into the night.

The two of them rushed off to Violet's house. When they got there, Violet threw on a sweater and earmuffs that were conveniently resting on the arm of her mother's whatnot chair. Then they snuck out of the house, being careful not to step on Alicia, who was snoozing on the floor in front of the television set.

Now they were ready to begin their quest. They headed straight to Minderbinder's. Thomas wasn't certain McGrowl would even be there, but it did seem a logical place to begin the search. He was having a hard time getting Violet's fur coat theory out of his head.

What, he wondered, were those two up to? And what use could they possibly have for McGrowl?

Thomas held the little heart-shaped dog tag tightly in his fist and ran his thumb down its ragged edge. He didn't know why, but a familiar image of an old woman who smelled like flowers popped into his head. And then he started worrying about McGrowl all over again. Where was he?

Thomas listened for a sign of some kind from the dog. He concentrated with all his might, but the place in his head reserved for incoming telepathic messages was disturbingly blank.

What Thomas didn't know was that the dog couldn't send him a message. He couldn't jump out a window, and he couldn't pull down a wall, either. He couldn't climb a tree if his life depended on it. At that very moment, McGrowl was trapped in Doc Minderbinder's basement. And there was absolutely nothing he could do about it.

The doctor had devised a devilish contraption that robbed McGrowl of his newly minted powers and reduced him, temporarily, to a friendly, rather obedient, and completely ordinary dog. At the moment, he was chained to a radiator, scratching a particularly irritating flea that had taken up residence on his left haunch and wondering when dinner would be served.

When Nurse Leona had slipped the metal chain over McGrowl's head and led him away from Thomas's house, Thomas and Violet had failed to notice a thin wire cable threaded through its links. The wily nurse intended to use the doctor's newest invention — a portable antielectromagnet. By pressing firmly on the side of her tote bag, she triggered a switch that activated a stream of powerful but invisible electrons. These subatomic negative particles streamed through the wire cable that ran around the dog's neck, temporarily undoing McGrowl's amazing abilities.

Rumors of the cataclysmic event at the power plant had reached the doctor, and when he witnessed the dog's amazing prowess, he quickly put two and two together. In this case two and two added up to a whole lot more than four.

Why was a dog, even a dog with super-powers, so important to a somewhat unorthodox veterinarian? The doctor needed the dog because he had a plan. He was going to take over Cedar Springs.

He had hatched his wicked plan when he was a small child. Minderbinder, whose actual name was Milton Smudge, was born under a dark star.

Some people are just born bad. Milton was one of those people. He stole from the class treasury and never, ever brushed his teeth. He resented other people when they were happy and decided that when he grew up he would make everyone's life as miserable as possible. So far he was doing a pretty good job.

The doctor was patient. He would accomplish his monstrous goal one block at a time.

As Doc Minderbinder stood on the landing at the top of the stairs leading down to the dark little basement where McGrowl was hidden, he felt a surge of excitement. He would achieve his goal. He felt certain. Once he harnessed the unlimited and amazing powers of a dog like McGrowl, nothing and no one could stand in his evil way.

He put an arm around Nurse Leona's shoulder and gave it a little involuntary squeeze. The gesture signified how happy, how absolutely mad with power the doctor felt to be standing on the brink of complete and utter domination of the town.

It certainly didn't signify the beginning of a new and glorious phase in their relationship, as Nurse Leona mistakenly assumed.

"Congratulations, Smudgie." The nurse beamed.

The doctor enjoyed neither the nickname nor the familiarity of the tone in which the round woman spoke.

"If you ever call me that again, you'll be out on the street so fast you won't know what happened to you."

Nurse Leona decided to think of the criticism as affectionate banter.

And then the doctor rushed outside to finish preparing a large rectangular box that was sitting, half completed, in the middle of the tiny backyard behind the offices.

Doc Minderbinder grabbed a handful of specialized tools, many of which had been designed by him in his very own laboratory, and started working feverishly to complete the contraption that took up most of the yard. It resembled a large cage, which indeed it was.

It was quite sturdy and weighed at least a ton. Between its thick metal bars, evenly spaced, hollow aluminum tubes ran up and down and sideways, every couple of inches. A series of cables, just like the ones that ran through the leash Nurse Leona had put around McGrowl to disable him, ran through the tubes. A massive extension cord snaked its way from the side of the cage over to yet another, much larger antielectromagnet.

Clearly, the doctor intended to put something tremendously powerful inside that cage and was taking great precautions to ensure that once it was in, it would never escape. Poor McGrowl. What a terrible series of coincidences had conspired to bring him to Doc Minderbinder's that fateful night.

If only he hadn't encountered Thomas and

Violet in the ravine. If only it hadn't been raining. If only Mr. McCarthy's truck hadn't run over the dog. If only the real Doc Minderbinder hadn't been sent out of town on a wild-goose chase, enabling a wicked impostor to move effortlessly into his office and take over his life.

The nameless stranger Thomas had come to distrust was not a doctor of any kind. He was brilliant, and he knew a lot about medicine, but that was where the similarities ended. When you are planning to take over your city, you make it your business to know a lot about everything.

Doctors want to heal the world and make it a better place. The stranger posing as Doc Minderbinder wanted to control the town for his own nefarious purposes and didn't much care who or what was injured along the way.

The impostor had done a topographical study of the neighborhood and discovered that the real Doc Minderbinder's office was sitting directly on top of what appeared to be one of the largest untapped deposits of oil and shale in the Midwest. He decided, then and there, that a well was to be dug. If, indeed, oil was as plentiful as the study indicated, he would simply find a way to get rid of the vet forever. He would then use the money from the well to help fund his dastardly efforts.

Nurse Leona, who was no more a nurse than he was a doctor, was disguised as a game-show host and sent to Doc Minderbinder's office with an urgent message. She informed the kindly doctor that he was the lucky winner of an all-expenses paid vacation to French Lick, Indiana, a delightful although isolated spa about seventy miles north of Cedar Springs. She punctuated the announcement by pulling out a small plastic trumpet from her purse and playing a few bars of "Hail to the Chief" very badly.

The doctor and his charming wife, the message continued, had been selected in a random drawing from all the veterinarians in the area and their immediate families. If Doc Minderbinder had had his thinking cap on, he might have realized that he was the only veterinarian in the area.

It might have also occurred to him that when game-show hosts arrive at your doorstep carrying prizes, they are generally accompanied by a television crew. But excitement had momentarily blinded the kindly doctor, and neither he nor his wife registered anything but happiness at the prospect of a free vacation.

Nurse Leona pulled out the trumpet again and foolishly attempted to complete "The Flight of the Bumblebee" in less than sixty seconds, damaging her lip in the process. Exhausted and no longer able to speak, she handed the enthusiastic couple an oversized check and the keys to the town of French Lick, which were, in truth, the keys to absolutely nowhere.

The doctor and his wife were off like a shot. Meanwhile, the ersatz doctor, who was hiding behind a nearby tree during the entire presentation, and the ersatz Nurse Leona moved in like a couple of mockingbirds. They were masters of disguise and had, through the clever application of makeup and certain prosthetic devices, turned themselves into reasonable facsimiles of the actual doctor and his wife, the real Nurse Leona.

Night was falling. Thomas and Violet took the shortcut past the library and were practically galloping when Thomas's seven-year-old cousin, Stuey Wiggins, and his mom, Molly Wiggins, turned the corner and nearly ran right into them.

"Stuey, tell Thomas where you've just been."

The last thing in the world Thomas needed

to hear about was the incredibly long and boring story of his Aunt Molly's trip to an Indian reservation in Minnesota.

But Thomas knew better than to rush his aunt. She was basically nice, but when she had a story to tell, nothing could bring her to an early conclusion.

Thomas just stood there and waited for the story to wind down. He gritted his teeth and worried about McGrowl.

CHAPTER TEN
Escape

While Thomas impatiently listened to his aunt's mind-numbing stories, McGrowl labored inside the cage that prevented his escape. The dog had been taken into the yard and shoved unceremoniously into his prison. The evil doctor removed the chain from around his neck, and in the twitch of a whisker, McGrowl felt his tremendous strength return.

He was ordered to dig a deep but narrow hole until some kind of black, wet, and extremely valuable substance was reached. McGrowl didn't want to obey the unpleasant man with the pinched face and bony fingers. He lay down and clenched his teeth and stubbornly refused to dig until Nurse Leona popped her head out a back window and smiled winningly.

"You better get off your you-know-what and get back to work, you filthy mutt."

She explained that something dreadful beyond imagining would happen to his pals if he didn't. The dog decided to do exactly as he was told.

"If you don't watch your step," warned the doctor, narrowing his already beady little eyes into terrifying slits, "the antielectromagnet will be turned up so high that your very atomic structure will be compromised.

"In fact," the doctor added, lowering his voice to a fiendish rattle, "you might end up a fish, or worse, even, a worm that gets eaten by a fish." The doctor shuddered with pleasure at the terrible thought. McGrowl tried not to listen and put more energy into his digging.

BEWARE OF DOG

Meanwhile, Nurse Leona worked cheerfully in the kitchen. It was the doctor's birthday, and she was assembling a large and especially gooey banana cream pie to celebrate the occasion.

She planned to surprise him with a little party in the garden. Nothing fancy. She purchased paper hats and blowers and a few surgical gloves, blown up and inscribed with festive greetings for decorations. No friends were invited, since neither of them had any.

The dog was already several hundred feet below ground level and busily digging away when he suddenly made a simple but important decision. If Thomas and Violet were in even the slightest bit of danger, he must try to escape.

He started digging furiously, sideways instead of downward. Earth and bits of roots went flying in all directions. Within a couple of seconds, the dog found himself well beyond the walls of his cage. He rocketed triumphantly to the surface, emerging somewhere near the back door, right underneath Nurse Leona. She had just completed putting the candles on the birthday pie and at that very moment was carrying it proudly out to the doctor.

She was about to yell "Surprise!" when McGrowl burst through the grass beneath her, sending her and her creation flying into the air. Instead of "Surprise!" she screamed a different, highly unprintable word. First the pie and then the woman herself made a crash-landing right on top of the unsuspecting doctor.

McGrowl couldn't have planned it better. The doctor was knocked unconscious from the blow and lay flat on the grass, covered in mounds of gooey whipped cream. Nurse Leona was in such a state of shock from her unintended fall that all she could do was sing "Happy Birthday" over and over as she lay covered by a mixture of bananas, cream, and grass.

McGrowl didn't waste a second. He grabbed his metal leash and, using both tooth and paw, swiftly tied it around the doctor and the nurse. He wrapped the end of the leash securely around a railing. And before leaping the backyard fence in a single bound, took a large and defiant bite of the pie, which he immediately spit right back out. Nurse Leona was a terrible cook. The dog could have saved himself a lot of trouble by simply letting her give the pie to the doctor, who probably would have died of food poisoning.

McGrowl hurtled down the street. He had to find Thomas. His legs moved faster and faster until he was an energized ball of fur that barely touched the ground. A trail of fallen leaves churned in his wake.

The poor, tormented cat, newly recovered

from her most recent run-in with the dog, had finally gotten up the courage to venture outside. She saw McGrowl barreling toward her at the speed of light and simply gave up. Escape, she decided, was not in the cards, and so she sat forlornly in the middle of the sidewalk and awaited her destiny.

The cat rubbed her eyes with her paws when the dog whizzed past, not even stopping to bark. At first she was greatly relieved, and then she began to wonder if she was losing her appeal.

Thomas sensed McGrowl vividly. He could see the dog running toward them as clearly as if he were looking directly into a window. He was so relieved he let out an involuntary whoop.

Aunt Molly didn't notice, and Stuey didn't care. Neither of them even batted an eyelash when the roar of an approaching tornado told

Thomas and Violet that McGrowl was, indeed, on his way.

Thomas greeted the dog with a sustained hug that was met with a flurry of licks and happy barks.

Poor Violet got in the way of the dog's tail, which was wagging so quickly that small trees were swaying from the draft it created. She blew backward down the street. Luckily, just as her feet started to leave the ground, she was able to grab onto a nearby fire hydrant. McGrowl and Thomas engaged in a brief but intense communication.

"Share, please," Violet said.

"We gotta get to Minderbinder's. It's worse than we thought."

"F-f-f-fur coats?" Violet stammered, her eyes widening.

Before Thomas had a chance to reply, McGrowl started racing down the street.

Thomas and Violet could scarcely keep up with the dog, who was traveling at a fraction of the speed of which he was capable. The dog didn't mind. He was happy to be reunited with his friend and with Violet. With his super-powers fully restored, he looked forward to capturing the evil stranger and his accomplice and bringing them to justice.

As McGrowl and Thomas and Violet neared the Minderbinder clinic, they slowed to a quiet tiptoe and carefully approached the building from the side. They needn't have been so careful. In a second they noticed the wide-open door, swinging back and forth lazily on its creaking hinges. All the lights in the house were out. Clearly no one was home.

And clearly little Susie and little Cicely — McGrowl's "rightful owners" — were a creation of the doctor's twisted imagination.

Before the anxious trio had even a second

to settle on a plan, McGrowl's superhearing detected the bending of some blades of grass. The dog and his friends turned around just in time to find the doctor and nurse standing calmly behind them, a large net in their outstretched arms. Violet let out a scream like a banshee. Before they had a chance to take a step, the net was hurled, and the children and their dog were being dragged back into the house.

Violet started screaming for help, and Thomas tried to grab onto Nurse Leona's legs, almost managing to trip her. McGrowl felt his powers diminishing the second he came into contact with the net. It had a series of tiny metal wires carefully woven into it and was, of course, connected to the dreaded antielectromagnet in Nurse Leona's tote bag.

Nurse Leona didn't even bother to hum. No one would have heard her. And anyway, the pesky children and their dog would soon be carefully locked away inside the house, never to be seen again.

The doctor and nurse pushed and pulled at their prisoners, working the net and its contents closer and closer to the doorway, as Thomas, Violet, and McGrowl tried frantically to break loose.

The dog grabbed a handful of the netting with his mouth and desperately started chewing on it. He would happily sacrifice himself if only he could create a hole large enough for the children to get through. He managed to break through one or two of the strands. But the strength in his jaws was so diminished he would have had a hard time with a steak, let alone yards of metallic wires.

They were almost inside the house now. Thomas and Violet and McGrowl didn't stand a chance against the two adults.

The doctor was grunting and sweating as

BEWARE OF DOG

Nurse Leona held the door open. They tried with all their might to push their captives through the doorway, into the house. Both Thomas and Violet stretched out their legs and arms and tried to form a living wedge too wide to get through the doorway.

"You might as well give up. Nothing can save you now. The dog is mine." The doctor was breathing so hard he could scarcely get the words out. Still he managed a terrifying and utterly mirthless laugh. It was clear that in another second the children and the dog would be overpowered and dragged into the house to face a fate Thomas didn't even want to think about. McGrowl knew this, too, and so he did the only thing he could think of.

He moaned and shuddered and stood up dramatically and then keeled over as if he were dead. Poor Thomas was so upset he almost started to give the dog CPR but received a quick message to back off. He realized that McGrowl was once again coming to the rescue.

As soon as McGrowl keeled over, the fake vet yelled at the fake nurse. She was so upset she started weeping and dropped her end of the net, allowing the two children and the dog to make a break for freedom. And then Nurse Leona called the doctor a name, and he started yelling at her. Then, suddenly, they both noticed their net was empty. Their captives had made it to the sidewalk and were making a mad dash for the alley that ran behind the houses across the street. The three escapees raced down the alley with their angry pursuers hot on their heels.

Where was Aunt Molly when you needed her? Thomas thought. He looked up and down the street and could see no trace of her or anyone else. He doubted the evil man would do any harm to them if somebody was watching. Thomas was correct. The doctor depended on anonymity. You couldn't take over a small shop, let alone an entire town, if people knew what you were up to.

Unfortunately, it was just that time of the evening when everyone was at home doing the dinner dishes or watching their favorite television show. There wasn't a person in sight.

The sound of pursuing footsteps was getting louder and louder. Fortunately, McGrowl felt his powers quickly returning. Strength surged through his body until he practically quivered. McGrowl quickly assessed the situation. After screeching to a halt, he grabbed Thomas by the belt and sent him a message to hold onto Violet with all his might. McGrowl bounded upward, pulling Thomas and Violet with him. Just then the evil duo turned into the alley.

"Stop, stop," Minderbinder screamed. "I

don't want to hurt you. I just want to be your friend" — as if there were the shred of a chance McGrowl, Thomas, and Violet didn't know exactly what kind of menace they were dealing with.

Violet felt the bottom of her stomach do a little dance as they flew higher and higher into the air. Thomas held his breath and summoned up the courage to look down. He was thrilled to see the doctor and his nurse far below them, rushing willy-nilly on the ground.

The strangers raced off in search of their prey. They couldn't imagine how their captives had managed to disappear into thin air, which was, of course, exactly what they had done. It never even occurred to them to look up. And then, McGrowl and the kids made a swooping descent, landing on exactly the spot where they had taken off. Thomas was panting so hard he could barely speak, but he managed to get out a warning to Violet.

BEWARE OF DOG

"Whatever you do, don't tell your mother. She'll never let you out of the house again."

Violet was in complete agreement. "I'm not even supposed to watch MTV."

McGrowl cast a bionic eye in all directions. Minderbinder and Leona were nowhere to be seen. All that remained of them were a pair of broken spectacles and a pom-pom from the top of Nurse Leona's favorite hat.

McGrowl immediately took a careful sniff of his archenemies' possessions. If evil had an odor, this was it. The dog practically reeled from an aroma that combined the scents of dead fish, greasy potatoes, and rhubarb with a distinct blend of formaldehyde and gasoline. This was a scent he would remember for a lifetime.

Thomas and Violet trailed behind as McGrowl led them quickly away. It was no longer safe being on the street.

As luck would have it, Officer Nelson,

Officer Ericson's newly installed replacement, happened to turn the corner at that instant, and the dog and Thomas and Violet ran right into him. Literally.

"Whoa, what's the rush, kids?" Officer Nelson picked himself up and brushed off his uniform. He smiled at Thomas and Violet and gave McGrowl a friendly pat on the head. If he had spoken to Officer Ericson before his rapid departure for the dude ranch, the pat might not have been quite so friendly.

And then McGrowl did the only thing he could think of. He hopped right through the open window of the officer's waiting police car.

"Hey, what's that dog doing?" Officer Nelson asked, bewildered. McGrowl had decided to try to beat the evil doctor and nurse back to their office. They were likely to return to their safe haven, and McGrowl looked forward to heading them off at the pass.

CHAPTER ELEVEN
The Encounter

In a minute the dog, his friends, and the officer were racing to Minderbinder's office, and Thomas was attempting to explain the story of the kindly vet, who wasn't really so kindly, and the heavyset nurse, who wasn't the angel of mercy she appeared to be. McGrowl filled in the details with a series of barks and growls.

Officer Nelson had no idea law enforcement in a small town could be so exciting. He was dedicated, eager, and proud to be the youngest member of Cedar Springs' tiny police force.

The officer radioed ahead to some colleagues in Green Haven and told them to get to the wily vet's office "pronto."

He thought about running home and looking for the bulletproof vest he had recently purchased. He made a swift decision to forgo the safety measure and concentrate on getting to the scene of the crime quickly.

Officer Nelson's car swerved around the corner and came to an abrupt halt about a block away from Minderbinder's.

"You kids stay in the car," he said protectively. "And keep your heads down."

Four uniformed detectives were waiting for the officer at the scene of the crime. They covered him as he ducked down and edged forward across the front lawn.

The policemen huddled in front of the large window and stared into the living room. The house was quiet and dark, except for a little night-light that burned softly in a corner. Officer Nelson was becoming light-headed, and it occurred to him he might actually pass out from the excitement of his first arrest.

Thomas and Violet and McGrowl got out of the policeman's car and silently joined the officers. They crouched quietly behind them, in front of the window. They waited for something to happen, careful not to make a sound. McGrowl's stomach gave out a rumble that was soon followed by the arrival of a now familiar odor.

The officers gave each other funny looks, and one of them even held his nose. Thomas controlled an urge to laugh. Violet didn't think it was funny.

And then a tall, thin man could be seen creeping down the stairs. Evidently, the evil duo had returned to their roost, and the man was sneaking into the kitchen to get something to eat. He was followed by his heavyset, diminutive partner. She wore a fuzzy pink robe and giant bunny slippers. What in the world, Thomas thought, were these two up to? Every muscle in McGrowl's body prepared itself to spring into action in case the doctor and his nurse should decide to escape. The officers stood ready, holding their breath in anticipation.

All of a sudden, the doctor flicked a switch in the kitchen, and the house was flooded with light. Thomas and Violet leaped back, startled, and even McGrowl looked uneasy. The doctor and his nurse heard the commotion and turned to look outside the window. They couldn't help but notice five police officers, two youngsters, and a large dog lined up directly outside their window. They tiptoed forward to see what in the world was going on.

"Freeze!" Officer Nelson shouted, frightening McGrowl, who barked loudly.

BEWARE OF DOG

Officer Nelson, unaware until now of the presence of the children and the dog, practically jumped out of his skin and nearly shot himself in the foot. The pajama-clad occupants of the house froze obediently, while the police attempted to look organized and professional.

McGrowl sniffed the air and noticed immediately that the repugnant scent of the doctor and the smell of cheap perfume that floated around the nurse were noticeably absent. But before McGrowl could communicate this to Thomas, Officer Nelson whispered under his breath, "Are those the bad people, son?"

"Yes, Officer. I'd know them anywhere," Thomas replied speedily.

That was all the eager young policeman needed to hear. Before McGrowl could do a thing about it, the officer leaped through the open window. McGrowl tugged at Thomas's pants and did his best to let him know this was all a mistake of gigantic proportions. Somehow the noise and the excitement seemed to make any thought transmission impossible.

The officer had the perfectly innocent and very real Doc Minderbinder and his wife on the floor in a flash, hands tied behind their backs.

It was then that Thomas realized something: The tall man and the fat woman certainly looked like Doc Minderbinder and his nurse, but when he concentrated really hard on the faces, he realized they were not one and the same. The doctor and his nurse resembled their doubles only superficially. Their eyes exuded a jolly glow. Thomas noticed that even under these dreadful circumstances, the creases on the sides of their mouths turned resoundingly up — nothing like the sour countenances of their predecessors.

Thomas would have laughed, except a feeling of dread hung over him like a black umbrella. He remembered suddenly that the evil duo who had replaced the doctor and his wife had vanished. They were nowhere to be seen. Who knew under what clever disguise they might surface again? Or if they were gone for good? Thomas seriously hoped this was the case. But deep in his heart he knew he would encounter the evil duo again.

"I think I've made a mistake, Officer."

While Thomas and Violet attempted to concoct an explanation for taking five police officers on a wild-goose chase, a shadowy figure lurked behind a nearby tree.

The thin, motionless man watched the proceedings as the fat woman stood beside him, equally still. They went unnoticed by everyone, including McGrowl, who would have identified their scents immediately, except for the fact that the local bakery was preparing the next morning's cinnamon buns.

The villains watched patiently. They were prepared to wait.

The officers apologized repeatedly as they untied the real Doc Minderbinder and his wife. Thomas wondered if he would be arrested for turning in a false alarm. His fears evaporated when the ungagged and unbound vet and his nurse started laughing merrily.

They stood up, brushed themselves off, and then warmly offered everyone's pets a free visit to the vet as they served them all steaming mugs of hot cocoa with marshmallows. Even McGrowl was given a bowl.

When every marshmallow was eaten and the last cup of cocoa slurped, McGrowl started herding Thomas and Violet away from the house. Thomas cocked his head to one side and listened intently.

"He's trying to tell us something."

"Hasn't he done enough talking for one

day?" It had been the longest day in Violet's life and she was getting cranky.

"McGrowl is tired, and he wants to go home."

"Me, too," Violet replied firmly.

The children said good-bye, and Officer Nelson thanked them for being so vigilant. He didn't mind the false alarm at all. He knew Thomas was a good kid who had meant well. Actually, he was a little relieved not to have run into a serious criminal first time out. Little did he know how close he had been standing to an evil schemer who planned to take over not only his precinct but the entire town.

Officer Nelson was kind enough to drive Thomas and Violet and the dog back to their neighborhood. It was cozy and warm in the car. Nobody said a word. The dog lay on his side in the back and encouraged Thomas to scratch his belly. Violet fell asleep twice, but

M^cGROWL

Thomas was so nervous he couldn't sit still. His thirty-six-hour deadline was up, and instead of finding McGrowl's rightful owner, he had spent most of his waking hours fighting evil. He couldn't imagine how he would ever get his mother to extend the deadline, let alone grant him his real wish — to allow McGrowl to stay with him forever.

CHAPTER TWELVE
AD at Last

They dropped Violet off first. A moment later, when the officer arrived in front of Thomas's house, McGrowl barked furiously and wagged his tail so fast Thomas thought he might take off like a helicopter. The dog was so excited to be back at the Wiggins's house, he raced up and down the inside of the police car like a wild hyena.

"Down, boy," Thomas said forcefully.

The dog paid absolutely no attention and continued running about.

"Cookies and milk to any dog who sits still and holds his breath," Thomas whispered discreetly.

McGrowl dropped to the floor like a sack of bricks.

"That's quite some animal you have there, son." The officer smiled as he got out and opened the door for the boy and the dog. Thomas couldn't have agreed more. He waved at the policeman, and then he and his new pal walked slowly up the path to the Wiggins's front door.

McGrowl was content. The evil doctor was out of commission, at least for the moment. And although he still missed the smelly old lady, he sensed somehow that she would be all right. He had a strong feeling that he would be seeing her again.

This was his new home, he felt certain of that. He couldn't wait to fall asleep next to Thomas. He felt so comfortable with him.

BEWARE OF DOG

Thomas was like a brother. A brother who walked on two legs and didn't have yellow fur, but a brother nonetheless.

By the time Thomas approached his front door, Mrs. Wiggins was about to telephone Mrs. Shnayerson. Then she noticed Thomas tiptoeing into the house. McGrowl was right behind him.

Mrs. Wiggins didn't even look up. She simply reminded her son that the thirty-six-hour deadline was fast approaching, and perhaps he ought to pack a bag for his doggy friend.

Thomas was certain there was one amazing thing he could say that would forever change his mother's attitude about pets. Unfortunately, he had no idea what it was. "Think of something, think of something," he said to himself, over and over. His legs were trembling, and his knees were so weak he was having trouble remaining upright. And then

McGrowl decided to take matters into his own paws.

The dog looked around the house and made a dash for the kitchen. Mrs. Wiggins was so startled she didn't have a chance to protest. She followed the dog into the room, where she had recently stacked the dinner dishes.

McGrowl raced to the sink, and with a little help from Thomas, managed to wash each and every dish with lightning-quick speed. The soapy dishrag he held in his mouth practically flew across the surface of the messy plates and silverware. He dried them all by wagging his tail furiously, and in about five seconds he had put away each and every dish and pot and pan into the cupboards where they belonged.

Mrs. Wiggins was absolutely stunned. She leaned against the wall and wiped her hands on her apron over and over.

"My, my," she murmured about two dozen times.

And then, noticing the amazing effect his performance was having on Thomas's mother, McGrowl went for the big finale. He took out a broom and a dustpan and, holding one in his teeth and the other with his paws, went around the entire ground floor of the house in about thirty seconds, sweeping under every chair and rug and leaping into the air and removing the occasional cobweb from a hidden corner. Mrs. Wiggins would likely have extended an invitation based on this performance alone.

Then he did something so astonishingly wonderful that Mrs. Wiggins could contain herself no longer. McGrowl cleaned the windows. Each and every one. Clenching an old newspaper in his teeth and quickly drying the soapy wet windows with his shoulders and torso, he whirled around the living room so fast he could scarcely be seen. When he finished, the house gleamed from stem to stern. Not a dust ball or a piece of lint remained.

Thomas's mother dabbed at her joyful tears with a hanky, looked worshipfully at McGrowl, and finally spoke.

"What a dear dog. What are we ever going to tell your father?"

Thomas felt his heart leap. His mother would let him keep the dog, and somehow his father would learn to cope. He would remind McGrowl to stay away from Mr. Wiggins and make sure he was on his best behavior 24/7.

Mrs. Wiggins gave her son a big hug. Then, wonder of wonders, she reached down and gave McGrowl an extremely friendly pat right on the top of his head. The dog beamed with pride. What a good dog he must have been to deserve such an honor! And then Mrs. Wiggins hurried off to try to think of something to say to Mr. Wiggins.

BEWARE OF DOG

Thomas brushed his teeth first and then took out a spare toothbrush and brushed McGrowl's.

As he brushed, he could hear his mother and father arguing softly in their bedroom. "Serious discussion" is how his mother liked to refer to the process. He knew that if it took all night, she would have her way. When Mrs. Wiggins knew she was right, there was nothing you could do to shake her resolve. And regarding Thomas and the dog, there was no doubt whatsoever that she was right.

McGrowl explored the room carefully. Home, he thought to himself. I'm finally home. He memorized every nook and cranny of the little bedroom. Then the dog hopped up onto Thomas's bed and burrowed deeply into the blanket.

Tomorrow, Thomas thought, he and Violet would have company on their way to school. Life would never be the same. Never in his wildest dreams had he ever imagined this day would finally arrive. At long last After Dog, the period Thomas had always referred to as AD, had begun. Thomas got into his pj's and slipped into bed with the dog. Dog and boy lay side by side, staring up at the ceiling, lost in a million thoughts.

Thomas wondered whether McGrowl would ever locate the smelly old lady. He wondered if his father would ever stop being afraid of dogs.

Suddenly, a strong gust of wind blew a tree branch against the window and made a noise that caused the boy to sit up in his bed. McGrowl opened his sleepy eyes and cast a wary look around the room. Thomas wasn't sure, but he thought he could see a shadow creeping along the far wall.

McGrowl seemed to sense something was wrong, too, and growled softly, but then the shadow stopped moving. It was probably just a bird flying past a street lamp, Thomas thought.

He forced himself to lie back in his bed, and McGrowl moved even closer to him and put his paw firmly across Thomas's chest. Nothing bad would ever happen to this boy. Not while McGrowl was around.

Thomas looked over at the pile of yellow fur, his head firmly nestled in his pillow, and whispered a solitary word quietly into his ear.

"Friend," he said.

And then he fell asleep faster than he ever had in his entire life.

Bob Balaban is a respected producer, director, writer, and actor. He has appeared in *Close Encounters of the Third Kind*, *Absence of Malice*, *Deconstructing Harry*, *Waiting for Guffman*, *Ghost World*, and *The Majestic*, among many other films. He has also appeared on *Seinfeld* as the head of NBC. Mr. Balaban produced and directed the feature films *Parents* and *The Last Good Time*, which won best film and best director awards at The Hamptons International Film Festival. He produced and costarred in Robert Altman's Oscar®-winning film *Gosford Park*, which was named Best British Film of 2001 at the British Academy Awards. Mr. Balaban lives in New York with his wife, writer Lynn Grossman, and his daughters, Hazel and Mariah. At the moment, he is canine-less, but he is looking forward to a close encounter with his own actual dog, not just one of the literary kind.